She Comes With Me

Rebekah Lynn

This is for the sinners who find salvation in each other, the outlaws who make their paradise, and the lovers who know that passion burns brightest in the dark. Welcome to a love story where loyalty is lethal, pleasure is power, and no one walks away untouched.

~Rebekah

Playlist

Flirt by NEFFEX
Inside Her Head by Bryce Savage
Mrs. Officer by Lil Wayne, Bobby V., Kidd Kidd
Unappreciated Queens by Georgiou Music
One Night by Jeris Johnson
Better Off by VOILÀ
BONNIE & CLYDE by Phix
Life's a bitch by TAELA
Never Too Late by Three Days Grace
Riot by Three Days Grace
Headstrong by Trapt
Last Resort by Papa Roach
Click Click Boom by Saliva
Burn It to the Ground by Nickelback
Bad Company by Five Finger Death Punch

Trigger Warnings

This book explores themes of heavy content, including but not limited to:

- Domestic violence (not between main characters)

- Miscarriage

- Sexual activity

- Narcissistic behavior

- Sexual assault (not between main characters)

- Breath play

- Improper use of prescription medication

- Sex trafficking

- Arrest

- Racial slurs

- Sex with someone other than the main characters

- Human auctions

- Death

- Stabbing

- Degrading behavior

Please be mindful of these and other potential triggers. If you find any of these topics distressing, prioritize your well-being and seek support if needed. Your mental health matters.

Chapter One

Alex

"What do you mean we leave in a week?" I scream into my phone. "That is barely any time to get my affairs in order for another damn deployment." I sigh. My Staff Sergeant isn't making this easy on me. We leave in a week, and we just got home a fucking month ago. I haven't even been able to get my dick wet yet. This is seriously some bullshit.

"García! Are you with me still?" My Staff Sergeant is pissed, not that I blame him. He must leave his pregnant wife and two boys at home to come on this damn deployment also. "Yes, Staff Sergeant, I am here with you. Just pissed at the last-minute changes to everything." I hate last-minute things. Welcome to the Marines, home of last-minute decisions, and hurry up and wait.

"Well, pass the word to everyone else that we will be leaving next week on Friday." Good god, I can't deal with this stupid last-minute bullshit right now. "Yes, Staff Sergeant, I'll send a group text for all the guys. Any word on where we are going?" Come on, Staff Sergeant, give me something good to work with. "Not yet; this is all the information Sir has given me. I will update you when I get more. Until that happens, I will spend time with my family." At least he has a family to go home to. I am a single Marine with no one to go home to... Guess I'll go to the bar with Smith tonight and see if we can get laid before we're in God knows where, doing God knows what. "No problem, Staff Sergeant. Enjoy your family. I'll talk to you later."

One week's notice. Fuck this shit- I need a drink. I pull out my cell, shooting off a text to the guys letting them know we are leaving soon and to get their shit in order. I opened Smith's contact and called him next. "Smith!" He answers on the second ring. "Hey, dude! Want to get drunk and get our dicks wet tonight?" I sigh into the phone. I am beyond irritated. We just got back a month ago... I am ready to just sit for five fucking minutes.

Is that even a thing? "Yeah, where are we going?" Smith is my right-hand man, always! "Let's go to Jill's Bar. I don't want to be around anyone we know tonight." Because who knows who will be around, and I don't need some dumb ass getting drunk and trying to start shit with me. I am in the mood to punch someone, and that's the last thing I need to see the captain for. It's not on my to-do list today. I need a beer and to throw some darts. "Sure, sounds good, dude! I'll meet you there at 6. I need a quick shower when I get home." I should also shower after my workout, which was ruined by a lovely phone call. "Yeah, I need to grab a shower also. I'll meet you there." I hang up because there's no need for goodbyes, and I love you to your buddy that you'll see in a few hours.

Once I get onto my black Harley-Davidson, I start it up and drive the five miles back to my house from the gym. I smell like ass. I do need to catch a shower. I decided I probably should call Ma and let her know that I am leaving again. I click on her name on the screen as I turn on the shower.

"Hola!" My mom sings on the phone. That singing always puts a smile on my face.

"Hey, Ma, I got some news. Are you, by chance, at home?" Let's hope she is so that she can sit down. She will not be happy with this news.

"Si, baby, I am making the bread, so I am home. What's going on?" Oh man, do I miss Ma's bread... I can already smell it from my memories.

"I am going back on deployment next week..." I winced while waiting for her to freak out. "Oh, baby, I am so sorry. I know you just got back and barely have any time to relax." I pulled the phone from my ear to give it a weird look. Well, that's not what I was expecting. Who is this lady, and where is my Mexican mom who always loses her shit?

"It's OK, Ma, it's what I signed up to do." She knows I went into the Marines because I wanted to do something good, but I know if I tell her how exhausted I am, she will freak out and want me to get out.

"OK, Mijo, if you say so. I worry about you. I will let your siblings know so that you can get ready to go. Te amo mi amor." God, this woman is the best. Always knows how to make me feel better.

"Love you too, Ma. I'll call you when I get the chance to." I hang up and get in the shower. God, I need a beer.

Once I get to the bar, I see Smith sitting with a beer already in his hand. I push through the crowd to get to him and sit with a flop on the bar stool. "What's up, dude?" I ask with a nod. He nods at me while taking a swig of his Budweiser. The bartender comes up to me with a short jean skirt, almost showing her ass cheeks, and a black tank top with her tits falling out. Man, I love this bar already! She leans a little forward, resting her arms on the bar top, bats her chocolate brown eyes at me, and says, "What can I get you, handsome?" with a bright white smile.

"Let's just start with a Bud heavy, please." She giggles and turns around. Her floral scent hits me in the face as I watch her straight, dark brown hair going halfway down her ass. She has curves in all of the right places, and I can imagine her being under me with her legs wrapped around my waist and her nails scratching down my arms.

"Hey dude, you OK?" Smith knocks me out of my day-dream and brings me back to reality.

"Yeah, I am good. I am just daydreaming. Probably need to get laid to get that under control." As I turn in my seat to face the bar again, the bartender comes up with my bottle of Budweiser and gives me a wink.

"The name is Ally. If you need anything else, give me a holler". She leaves with a sway in her hips that almost has me drooling.

"Ally is hot, man!" I hear Smith say over the music.

"I could totally get under that." I chuckle and nod.

"Yeah, me too." He agrees and takes another long drink of his beer. It doesn't matter who we get under tonight. We will be gone next week, and it will become a memory for our Spank Bank.

After a few hours, several beers, and three dart games later, Smith and I felt ourselves. So much so that he was trying to get Ally to have a threesome with him and me; she just laughed and shrugged it off like it was nothing. Little did she know that Smith was dead serious. This dude is always trying to have a threesome.

We go back to our game until we hear some yelling on the other side of the bar.

"What do you mean this is the best you got, Bitch!" That's all it took to turn around and see what was happening. I see some guy in Ally's face, yelling at her like she's street trash.

That will not happen when I am around. You will not disrespect a woman!

I nudge Smith while he is taking a swig of his beer and nod towards the commotion.

"You hearing this?" he nods, and you can see the rage in his eyes.

We stand and walk over to this tall man, probably about 6'2", with salt-and-pepper hair and a long beard. His face has enough wrinkles to show his age. He is wearing a cut-off jean jacket, jeans in a different color from his jacket, and black combat-style boots.

"Let's chat with our man who thinks he has enough balls to yell at a woman, shall we?" Smith cracks his knuckles in response.

We walk up behind Ally, who is visibly shaking in all of her five-foot-nothing self.

"Hey Ally, what's going on here?" I ask.

"Nothing, I'm fine." She says over her shoulder. You can tell she doesn't mean a word of what she says.

"Mhm... Sure doesn't look fine to me, Ally."

I look up at the man who hasn't said a word now that Smith and I are standing here. He snarls, puffing out his chest like he is big and macho.

"She said she's fine! So, take your beaner ass back to Mexico and take your cracker friend with ya!"

All I could do was laugh at his ignorance. Seriously, are we going to throw race into this? Little does he know, I may be Mexican, but I could crush his ass.

"Dude, you don't want to play the Mexican card with me." I roll my eyes and look back down at Ally, who is blankly staring at the wall. She is visibly shaking, and her face is as pale as a sheet.

"Who the fuck are you calling a cracker?" You hear Smith grumble from behind me.

"Oh, so you're a retard also?" The man's eyes glistened like he had just won. That is when I knew all hell was going to break loose.

"What the fuck did you say?" Xander says through clenched teeth. Xander doesn't like people being called dumb; definitely not retarded. It comes from his younger brother being autistic. People called his brother retarded and dumb all his life.

"Did I stutter?" The old man chuckles and looks back at his friends. That's when Xander jumped up and punched the guy in the face. His nose was now crooked from the break, blood gushing out of his nose and down his shirt.

Ally starts screaming at the top of her lungs and runs behind the bar.

Well, I can't let my man get himself killed right before we leave, so here goes nothing. I jump into the fight, bringing my fist to the old fuckers right cheek, and then swing for his beer gut! The man gets a good solid hit on my left cheekbone, my head snaps to the side, and rage feels my bones. I swing again and see the reflection of red and blue lights flashing outside. FUCKKKKKK, this is all I need right now.

Chapter Two

Olivia

Friday night shifts are always full of drunk people and fighting. When I entered the academy, I thought there would be more action. Carrying drunk people into the drunk tank every night is not my idea of fun.

When I was a teenager, I told my dad that I wanted to be a cop, and he laughed at me. My family is all in the Finance field. My dad and grandfather were bank presidents, and my Uncle and brother were CFOs.

Of course, I joined the Police force right out of high school, so they didn't try to bribe me to join the financial business. I didn't want to deal with money or sit behind a desk. I wanted to be involved in the action and make a difference.

As I drive, the radio screams at me, "We have a bar fight at Jill's bar on 5th Avenue."

"Unit 7639, en route," I reply to the dispatcher. Flipping on my lights, I head towards Jill's.

Well, we shall see how this night turns out—there's an assault happening at a bar. My guess is two guys fighting over who has the bigger dick. I roll my eyes and continue to speed the mile to the bar. Pulling up, I see a group crowded around one area inside the bar.

Well, they are predictable today. Let's hope they don't try to buck up to me just because I am a woman. I would love to put them in their place and show them what a real woman can do. I fucking hate being underestimated.

When I step into the bar, everyone turns and looks at me. In the background, someone says, "The po po are here."

I roll my eyes and keep walking toward the fight. Looking down, I see three men rolling around on the floor like pigs. I laugh and think to myself.

They call us the pigs.

"What's going on here?" I say, loud enough to be heard over the music. All three guys stand up and look directly at me.

A petite brown-haired girl comes toward me from the bar. She says, "The older one was yelling at me and calling me vulgar names, then these two came over to ask if I was ok, and the older one started throwing racial slurs at them, and the blonde one punched the old man in the nose, and the brunette jumped in also and it has been fists and blood flying everywhere."

This sounds like the most pathetic excuse to call the cops, but here I am. I take the statements of the girl and the two men involved. I will get to the witnesses after; I know their stories will be overdramatic and fabricated.

When I approach the last guy, my breath catches in my throat. He has the most beautiful brown eyes and dark brown hair. He is taller than me by a mile. I would guess he is pushing 6'6", but there's no telling when you sit at a solid 5'5" on a good day. His biceps are bulging through his black shirt, and you can see the delicious veins running through his arms. He smells like beer, Cedarwood, and sin. Holy hot damn, I need to take a step back; his smell alone is making me dizzy.

I take a small step back and raise my eyes to meet his.

"Can I get your name, Sir?" I say quietly, I swear it came out as more of a squeak than actual English.

He chuckled, and the deep rumble through his chest sent a warm feeling to my core.

"Yeah, it's Alejandro Lopez García. What's yours?" He says with a half-smile. That accent that he has will cause a girl to have a heart attack.

With an eye roll, I reply, "I am Officer O'Connor; now, please tell me what happened in your own words."

After an hour of being at the bar, I am finally on my way out with the man I now know as Xander Smith, handcuffed and being led to my car.

He happens to be the unlucky fucker who is being brought in for taking the first swing. If he had just let the old man talk his shit, he wouldn't be sitting in the back of my squad car right now, humming a tune as if he had no care in the world. I wish I could be in his head to know his thoughts.

I get into the driver's seat and buckle up, keeping to myself as I drive to the station. I pull him out of the car when we pull into the station, and he is still humming his tune. We walked in, and I started recording his personal information and gathering his belongings. Once the tedious paperwork is done, I take him to get his mugshot taken. Once the necessities are taken care of, we check to make sure he won't be a threat to himself or anyone else, and then lock him up to get sober for the night.

He said he didn't want to use his one phone call because Alex was the one he would call, and he knew where he was.

I sit at my desk, trying to fill out these reports from the assault and submit them, but all I can think about are those beautiful brown eyes staring into my soul, the same ones that will be haunting my dreams in the future. I shake myself out of my daydream and look up at the clock on the far wall. It was 2 am, and finally, it was the end of my shift, even though I hadn't accomplished anything that night after arresting Xander. The fight was the only call I got worth anything. I had a couple of speeding tickets and a guy who was nude running through the park.

A figure catches my eye as I walk out of the building. Immediately, I go for my 9mm pistol on my hip, ready for anything to happen. It's 2 am in San Diego; you never know what you will find on the streets.

As I approach the figure standing outside the gate, I can already feel those beautiful brown eyes on me. Then, the wind blows his woodsy smell toward me, invading my senses. My body goes into overdrive. What is Alejandro doing here? I look him in the eyes, and a warm feeling fills my chest. It feels so... right.

Before stepping any closer, I heard his voice call out to me. "Hey! Officer O'Connor!" I walk up to the fence and see Alejandro leaning against a barrier, taking a drag of his cigarette. He grins at me with his panty-dropping smile and then blows the smoke up in the air.

"What are you doing here, Alejandro? Xander won't be out until morning when he is sober." You would think he would know that.

"I'm not worried about Xander. Maybe a night behind bars will get him to calm his temper." He smiles at me with a shrug. It seems odd because I only saw the Xander that was humming the whole time, from the back of my squad car until I shut the gate to his cell for the night. He seems so peaceful.

I sigh. "If he isn't the reason you are here, then enlighten me about the reasoning. Because I know you didn't drive 10 mins from the bar to stand outside the station's gates for nothing."

Alex laughs a deep, contagious belly laugh. As much as I want to smile at him because his laugh is everything, I cock my eyebrow at him and cross my arms, tapping my foot as my patients run thin. He may be cute, but he's messing with my shower, reading with a glass of whiskey, and sleeping time. My nightly routine is a ritual. I'm on autopilot most of the time when I get off work. I don't want to have to think after dealing with these idiots all night.

Finally, he stops laughing and looks at me. "Well, first off, Ms. Officer, I didn't drive under the influence. I have more morals than that. I took an Uber. You know, the thing you request a car on to take you places."

I roll my eyes. "I know what fucking Uber is!" I damn near screamed at him. How can he be so handsome and so infuriating at the same time? I want to climb him like a tree and slap the smirk off his face all at the same time.

"Oh, good. I was nervous there for a second." He looks up at me with a cheeky grin and then continues.

"I came here after you took Xander. I couldn't get you off my mind, so I thought I would ask if you wanted to get some food with me at the diner down the road. It's open 24 hours, and I didn't know any other way to ask you out. So here I am going all in." He asked me to go to a diner on a date at 2 in the morning. Is he desperate or crazy?

"You want to take me out on a date, Mr. Lopez García?"

"Please don't call me that. That is my grandfather. Just call me Alex, " he says, looking shocked as if he had spilled some huge secret to me.

He takes another drag of his cigarette, nodding his head as he flicks the cherry of the cigarette on the ground, stomps it out, and throws away the butt. Hmmm, usually smokers throw their butts on the ground. I am shocked to see he cares for the environment.

"Wow, I have never met a man who gets turned on by watching his friends get arrested. Was it the handcuffs or the manhandling that did it for you?" I wink at him and chuckle.

"Both; I wouldn't mind being manhandled and put in cuffs by you. And when I say you, I mean only you!" Then he winks at me and walks towards the diner, not even turning around to see if I am following. The cocky fucker knew I would go with him. I am not sure how he can read me so well already, but I don't like it.

Chapter Three

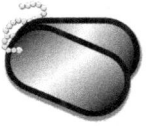

Alex

I would be lying if I didn't say the world stopped when Officer O'Connor entered the bar. My breath stopped, and my eyes could only focus on her. It was intense, as if the world had started and stopped with her. I had never felt that way before; honestly, it was terrifying.

Her beauty was unimaginable, from her long auburn hair to her blue/green eyes and her plump lips that I could see wrapped around my cock. She was sitting at maybe 5'5". Short, but she was strong. You couldn't tell by her body type; she was lean, but it was clear she worked out regularly.

A woman with muscles has never turned me on! But the way she manhandled the shit out of a drunken Smith was sexy as fuck. That was also some shit that I will never let him live down!

So, what is the only thing my mind can think of after she takes Smith to the cop cruiser? Her!

I got an Uber to take me to the police station. Yes, I am taking an Uber to the police station; desperate times call for desperate measures! And I am a man desperate to know Officer O'Connor's first name. Maybe she will agree to a date; if not, I'll just take the first name and go for more later. Fuck, why am I even worried about a date and getting to know her better when I leave soon? This girl has gotten into my head!

I stood outside the station for almost two hours. I sound pathetic, but I wasn't paying for another Uber to leave when I had already spent money to get here. So, I light up a smoke and scroll through social media to see what is happening in the real world. I hate all the bullshit that is on social media; the only reason I have it is to keep up with friends and family when I am gone.

As soon as I hear the click and the squeak of hinges -that could use some WD-40- I look up from my phone, take another drag of my cigarette, and smile. Good god, she is gorgeous! Her pale skin glowed under the street-lamp, her eyes shining from the moon, and I would rec-ognize that red hair anywhere! I adjust my pants, which are now significantly more uncomfortable, and scream out, "Hey! Officer O'Connor!"

After much convincing, she agreed to have dinner —or was it breakfast now, given how early it was? Who fuck-ing knows; all I know is it's a win in my book to have this gorgeous woman sitting across from me at this shitty diner; that smelled like pancakes, coffee, stale beer, and body odor. The only people here are drunks trying not to have a hangover the next day and truckers who are stopping for a quick bite.

"I have never been here," Officer O'Connor said, looking around.

"This is where I go to get waffles when I am drunk and need to soak up the alcohol." I looked at her slowly, trying to gauge the situation before revealing my whole personality. Many people have told me that I'm a lot to handle; I like to think I'm just enough for the right person.

"Also, it would be cool to know your first name so I can stop referring to you as Officer O'Connor." A small chuckle leaves my throat in embarrassment. Why the fuck am I embarrassed? That's not a thing I do! What is it about this girl that is catching me off guard with everything I am doing? This was supposed to be just an attempt at a casual hookup before I left again.

"My name is Olivia, but watching you squirm while you call me Officer O'Connor is funny, so I thought I would enjoy it a little longer." She has a mischievous grin on her face. Man, she has a smart-ass mouth on her. I would love to spank the smart ass out of her!

"What can I get you two this morning?" The waitress asked, shaking me out of my thought of Olivia's ass being red with my handprint. I have to shake my head to get the dazed look out of my eyes.

Olivia looks up to her first. "Yeah, please, I'll have a black coffee and some bacon." That's it? That's all she will eat after a complete shift of work?

"I'll have the same," I tell the waitress. She winks at me and then heads to the next table.

"So tell me, Alex, what do you do for work, and how do you know Xander?" I knew this conversation was coming. How do I know the crazy drunk who punched an old man first? "We are both in the Marine Corps," I said, giving the basics. I don't want to scare her away too quickly. They run as soon as I tell anyone I am a Marine. That, or they want to get married yesterday. Being in a relationship or married to someone in the military is not for the faint of heart. We are always shipped off to do stuff at random times. But people think the benefits are worth it. That's why you hear about a lot of spouses getting cheated on while there is a deployment.

The waitress brings us our cups of coffee and a large silver thermos filled with more coffee, then turns around and walks away. I grab the thermos and give poor Olivia and me some coffee before she asks, "So, what do you do in the Marines?" I look up from my coffee. "We are infantry, so we are boots on the ground and rifles in hand, kind of Marines." She looks at me with shock at that answer as she takes a long drink of her coffee.

"Mmhmm." That's all you got? Mhm, is that all you can think of to say?

"Yeah, it's a demanding job; I assume you would know about demanding jobs since you are a police officer," I say sarcastically and laugh after to make sure she knows I am joking.

The conversations went on for two hours. We talked about random things, everything from our childhood to tonight's crazy incident to her love for being a cop. It was nice, relaxing, and comfortable.

When we finally decided we both needed to get some sleep, it was around 4:30 a.m.

I have a feeling that one of the guys will call me in two hours to ask me what's going on with this out-of-nowhere deployment. I don't even know where we are going. Maybe LT will know what's going on. Being a part of such a small group of people, you get close to all of your coworkers. I guess it's time to face this shit show.

"It has been an amazing morning. Thank you, Olivia, for gracing me with your presence for breakfast." I take a dramatic bow to her, curling one arm in front of me and the other behind me like a knight would do.

Olivia rolls her eyes and chuckles at me. "Thank you for inviting me out, Alex. It was a great time."

I pull up my Uber app to get a ride back to the house. Of course, this early in the morning, there is barely anyone driving, so I will have a thirty-minute wait. I look up to Olivia, who is watching me intensely.

"Do you want me just to give you a ride home?" She asks with a smirk on her face.

"Yeah, that would be great. I will give you some gas money." She laughs and shakes her head at me. "It's okay; you don't have to give me gas money. I really don't mind."

Wow, she is even cuter when she smirks! This girl is something else.

When we return to the station to get Olivia's car, we walk up to a new black-on-black Cadillac XT6. I swear, this girl keeps getting better and better! I can't even comprehend my thoughts right now. Overwhelmed with awe.

I whistle out, "Nice Car." This car screams sexy car for a sexy lady.

Chapter Four

Olivia

"Thanks?" I don't know what to reply to, 'Nice ride.' I mean, I know it's nice; I worked my ass off to get this car and pay it in full. I didn't want a damn car payment on top of everything else.

"So where am I going?" I am taking him home; that's where I'm going, then I'll go home and sleep. It has been a long night, and I'm still not used to swing shifts. I am more of a morning or night shift person. In my opinion, swings are for crackheads. I feel like I am always tired and can't get anything done throughout the day because I spend most of my time sleeping.

"I live by the base. Here, I'll pull it up on the GPS for you," he quickly types on his phone. Then, he sets it in the cup holder facing me so I can follow the directions it gives.

I turn the radio on to the Hip-Hop station. This station is my go-to for keeping me awake on my drive home.

Of course, the next song to come on was "Mrs.Officer" by Lil Wayne, and just as I went to change the station, Alex started singing the song! Surprisingly, he doesn't have a bad voice at all. Once he turns in his seat and starts singing directly to me, my cheeks heat up, and I blush like a teenage girl.

"That's it! We are done with this song." I change the station, and he laughs at me.

"Didn't like my singing?" he winked at me.

"It's not your singing that made me change the station. It was the song." I roll my eyes and turn it to some heavy rock. Yes, I know I have an odd taste in music.

Next to me, Alex starts to headbang to this new song I have never heard before. All I can do is watch and chuckle. This man is a goofball and gives no fucks who sees. That's a very admirable attribute.

As we drive through San Diego's streets, I tap my fingers on the steering wheel while Alex enjoys his rock band concert in the passenger seat. He plays air guitar, imaginary drums, and even the imaginary keyboard while continuing to headbang. I don't know how he isn't dizzy; I feel like I'm getting dizzy watching him.

We come up to a stoplight. I look to my right and see a guy screaming at a petite, blonde-haired girl. Her eyes are completely red, her hands are in her hair, pulling on her blonde locks, and she is shaking. I turn the music off and roll down my window just enough to hear what they say.

The poor girl sputtered out, " I'm sorry, Andrew... I'm so sorry!" The man she was with was about 6'2" with messy red hair and a red beard that didn't look like it had been maintained in months; he was wearing a band tee and jeans that looked like they had oil and grease all over them. You could see the rage as he flings his hands up in the air and starts to scream some more.

"You're sorry? That's all you have to say, you stupid bitch?" He pulls his arm back and slaps her across the face. The poor girl fell to her knees and broke down in tears. The red-haired guy that I heard is named Andrew, turns, and, with all of his weight, roundhouse kicks the girl in the stomach and makes her fly from her knees into the building they are standing next to. She buckles over, holding her stomach, trying to catch her breath.

"Did I just see what I thought I just saw?" Alex said as he unbuckled his seatbelt and opened the car door before I could answer him. He is in a full sprint toward the couple as soon as his feet hit the pavement.

The light finally turns green, and I pull over the car as fast as possible while dialing 911 to get an actual officer out here who is on duty. I need to get an ambulance and the police here.

Alex had the man's face against the wall, both arms behind his back. This Andrew dude was kicking and screaming incoherent things at Alex.

As I hung up with the dispatcher, I ran over with my handcuffs from duty. I came up behind Alex and placed a cuff on Andrew's wrist. Then, I took the other wrist from Alex's grip and handcuffed it.

"Go check on her." I move my chin toward the girl lying on the ground, holding her stomach. I could hear

Alex ask her if she could hear him and if she was okay as soon as he was in front of her. Reassuring her that the paramedics were coming to get her. He was so patient and caring toward her. It was so amazing that he had that compassion in such a shitty situation.

I turn to look back at Andrew with a glare. "She said she was pregnant." He tried to explain to me, as if that were an appropriate excuse to kick someone into a building.

"Shut the fuck up before I knock your ass out! You are on a very thin line right now, and it's taking all of my self-control to keep calm and not beat the living fuck out of you." I am fucking fuming right now!

"You can't, you are a pol..." I hold my hand up to cut off what he is saying. I know he thinks that because I still have my uniform on, that I wouldn't beat his ass. Little does he know, I don't give a fuck!

Fucking pregnant? He just kicked a pregnant woman in the stomach?

"Alex, is she ok?" I look over at Alex with the girl. From where I am standing, I can see a pool of blood under her; the back of her head is also busted; her blonde hair is in a knotted, bloody mess. She probably has a broken rib from how hard she was kicked. No one deserves this.

"She is beat up and says her stomach hurts, but that is expected when she just got kicked in the stomach." He said, while holding her in his arms and rubbing her hair to soothe her. He is covered in her blood

I interrupted him, "Ask her how far along she is." He looked at me, confused, and turned to ask her anyway.

"She said 12 weeks. How did you know she is pregnant?" I ignore him and turn back to Andrew.

"You know you are fucked, right?" He looks up at me and gives me a smug smile. I roll my eyes and turn to look at the girl.

As I looked up, I saw the ambulance lights rushing towards us. Thank God! This girl needs to go to the hospital right now!

Chapter Five

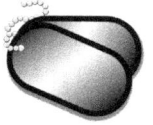

Alex

Rachel. That's this poor woman's name. She looks so broken and fragile, lying here in my arms, holding her stomach and sobbing. She has blood running down her face from the huge gash on her forehead down through her eyebrow. I am trying to soothe her as much as I can by rubbing her hair and telling her that the paramedics are on the way. I don't want to say it will be alright because, truthfully, I don't know if it will be. It threw me for a loop when Olivia asked me how far along she was. She doesn't look pregnant at all, but the big spot of red pooling below her can't be good for a pregnant woman. FUCK! Can the paramedics get here?

"Shhhhh, I got you, Rachel. I got you. Everything will be ok. I am here with you. I know you don't know me, but I will do anything you need me to do. We are just waiting for the ambulance to get here. You will be ok. I promise." She looks up at me. Her blue eyes are puffy and red from crying.

"Will you go to the hospital with me? I don't have anyone and don't want to be alone right now. I am not sure what to expect with my baby, but I feel like I know the answer." The shock on my face made her lips curl in the tiniest smile. I guess my emotions are all over my face right now.

"Yeah, I will go with you, Rachel. You won't be alone through this. By the way, I am Alex, and Olivia is the woman over there. She is a cop, so she called the on-duty cop to come and get Andrew." She just nodded. I feel worthless. All I can do is sit here and watch her. I can't stop the pain or bleeding; I can't stop the emotional hurt. I can't do fucking anything. But all I want to do is protect her and take away the pain.

I kissed her head without even thinking. As I looked up, I saw an ambulance coming towards us. Thank god. She needed the ambulance 30 minutes ago. I know they can't go any faster than they are, but I wish they could.

"Hey, sweetie, the ambulance is almost here. They will help you and the baby to the best of their abilities."

She looked up at me with complete terror on her face. "Aren't you coming with me?"

"Yes, love, I am. Don't worry, I will be coming with you. I need to step back and let the paramedics take care of you. I just wanted to let you know that I am still here and will stay as close as possible without interrupting the paramedics." She relaxed in my arms when the ambulance parked, and two paramedics jumped out. One exited from the back with a bag slung around his back, and the other was from the passenger seat.

They rush up to us, start pulling gloves out of their bags, and ask so many questions that it's hard to keep up. Rachel looks at them blankly but doesn't answer.

She starts to shake, and the paramedic yells at the driver, who is now working on getting the gurney out of the back, "She is going into shock!" The paramedic comes running over with a blanket while the one to the left starts to bend her legs.

"Sir!" I turn my attention back to the paramedic near Rachel's head, who is trying to talk to her.

"Yes? I am sorry. Can you please repeat what you said?" The paramedic looks from Rachel to me and asks. "Do you know what happened here?" I look up.

"Yes, that man over there–" I point to Andrew, "and Rachel were arguing when we were driving by. We heard the screaming and then saw him kick her in the stomach. She flew from right next to the road to this wall and hit her head; she then slumped to the floor." The paramedic then started to look at Rachel's head and began to touch where she has a large gash on the back of her head.

I turned to look at Olivia and realized the cops were also there. She was talking, and her hands moved with everything she said. There was rage in those green/blue eyes.

I look over at Andrew, who is getting a new pair of cuffs on his wrist. He is laughing like a lunatic. Why is he even laughing? This dude seriously has issues.

The officers lift Andrew, walk him to the squad car, and put him in the back.

Olivia is still talking to the other officer, taking her statement. They must have worked together because the officer spoke to Olivia as if they were friends and tried calming her down after she almost beat the shit out of Andrew.

As soon as I turn back around, they are lifting Rachel onto the gurney, and she is crying. Through the sobs, all I can hear is, "He is coming with me! Don't leave without him!" I assume she is talking about me.

I stand up, walk over to where she is, and grab her hand. She holds my hand in a death grip like she is scared she will fly away. "I'm not leaving you. I am right here." You can see her shoulders relax a bit. "Sir, are you coming with her?"

I look over at Olivia and then at the paramedic talking to me. "Yes, I am. Let me go tell Olivia that I am going with her."

I turn to walk towards Olivia as I glimpse the paramedic lifting his eyebrow at me. I roll my eyes and continue walking to Olivia. I touch her shoulder and say, "Hey, Rachel wants me to go with her. I just wanted to let you know before I leave." She turns towards me and nods.

"She needs someone with her. Keep her safe." I nod in response, head for the ambulance, and get in. I go straight to Rachel's side, grab her hand, lightly squeeze it, and smile.

We zoom through the San Diego streets, sirens blaring. Rachel is in and out of consciousness. "She is bleeding a lot. I need an OBGYN on-site! We are ETA, ten minutes out." The paramedic, who has been in the back the whole time, is saying things through his walkie-talkie.

We pulled into the emergency vehicle side of the ER, and a whole team of doctors and nurses was waiting for us. Rachel groans while they wheel her down the hall.

"Sir! Who are you? How are you related to the patient?" A nurse with a clipboard asks me.

"I am not related to her. I am the one who stopped to help her when her fiancé kicked her into a wall. She asked the paramedics who came to the scene if I could come with her. She has no one else." I say, rushing as I speed walk through the hospital halls, trying to keep up with everyone.

We finally stop in one of those stupid curtain rooms that aren't actually rooms, and I hear the doctors talking. I am not sure what they are saying, but I hear something about surgery, prep OR, and blood loss. I wish I could hear everything so I know what is going on.

I stare at Rachel, watching her chest rise and fall to make sure she is still breathing. I have so much anxiety right now with everything going on. She is not dying on my watch.

"Sir, Ms. Fayet has to go into surgery, and since her documents do not list her next of kin, I need you to sign these, giving us permission to proceed with the necessary surgeries." A male nurse with a computer on a cart comes up to me.

"Um. Is that even legal?" I ask, completely confused. I barely know this girl, and they want me to sign official documents on her behalf.

"Yes, sir, the paramedics heard her ask you to come. They said she started to panic when she thought you were not coming with her. So, if no next of kin is listed, the friend with them is the primary point of contact for medical decisions. And since Ms. Fayet is unconscious at the moment, this is handed to you." He says this like he is the fucking man who wrote the law. I don't have time to look up this information, so I have to trust what he is saying.

"Ok fuck it, what do I need to sign? Just save her life, please. I don't want anything to happen to her." I say as the computer signing pad gets handed to me to sign. I scribbled my signature on the line, and the nurse thanked me before leaving the room. I turn back to Rachel and stand beside her.

"I hope you aren't mad at me when you wake up for what I just did. I know they only want to save you; if I had the ability, I would save you myself. But unfortunately, there is already one Superman, and the bastard stole the position from me." I say with a chuckle.

I hear a noise from the curtain opening, and I look up. A tall, blonde nurse comes in, smiling like she just heard me make a fool of myself.

"Alright, sir. We are taking Ms. Fayet back for surgery now. You can wait in the waiting room," she says to me.

"How long should the surgery take?" I ask in a panic. I know this is necessary, but I don't want to leave Rachel alone. She trusted me to stay by her side the whole time.

"Honestly? I don't have an answer to that. We are going in for a life-saving surgery to stop the internal bleeding that is going on." She looks back at her notes on the clipboard and then looks back up at me with sympathy.

Then it dawns on me. "What about the baby? I thought women shouldn't have surgery while pregnant." I am no expert on pregnancy, but that would make the most sense to me.

"I'm so sorry, sir. The baby didn't make it. There was no heartbeat when she got here, and she was bleeding a lot. Unfortunately, the impact was too severe for the fetus to survive." She tells me as a tear rolls down her cheek.

"Thank you for letting me know. Please save Rachel. I don't want anything to happen to her." I comfort her by placing my hand on her shoulder. Her emotions tell me she loves and is deeply invested in her job. I know she will take care of Rachel with everything she has.

"We will do our best, sir." As she says this, she leaves the curtain room. A group of nurses enters and begins moving cords and IV bags, then unlocks the wheels to move the bed. It all happens so fast that I have no idea what's happening until she's gone.

I slide down against the wall, putting my face in my hands, only hearing the sound of monitors beeping and the smell of sickness and bleach. My mind is in over-drive, and I feel myself breaking down.

I look up to watch them wheel Rachel away. A piece of my soul felt like it left me as I watched her get wheeled down the hall.

Chapter Six

Rachel

I woke up with a headache from hell, cords attached to me, and the worst stomach pain I have ever experienced. I lift my arm to my head, feel the bandage wrapped around my head, hit myself in the face with the line of the IV in the crease of my arm, and I am in an ugly hospital gown.

Sitting in this uncomfortable bed, I try to recall what happened. I remember telling Andrew that I was pregnant, I remember him being pissed and slapping me across the face, and I remember the most beautiful brown eyes. But my head is so fuzzy I can't think straight, and my memories are choppy; I hope I regain my memory. I look around and see a man lying his head on the edge of my hospital bed. I jump because I realize it's not Andrews's head lying there; instead of greasy, red hair, it is silky brown, longer on top, and fading down to the skin on the sides. I reach out to touch him, and he jumps up before I can feel his hair; it looks so soft.

"Oh my god, I'm sorry! I didn't mean to fall asleep on your bed! I'm so glad you're awake. Let me get the doctor. How are you feeling?" His attack of questions and nerves is the cutest thing I have ever heard; it makes me smile. His Hispanic accent is the sexiest thing I have ever heard. I don't know how the sexiest voice I have ever heard said the cutest. It makes no sense.

"I..." It was all that squeaked out. My throat is sore; it feels like I swallowed sandpaper.

"Shhh, don't talk. It's ok. Let me get the doctor so they can check you. Then we will get you some water." He gets up and hurries to the door. I look around my room. It is a bare hospital room. A couch is in the right corner of the room, next to a large window. There is a sink across from my bed, next to a door that I assume leads to a bathroom. Then, there is the final door to the left, where the man went to get the doctor, so that would be the main door. The walls are plain beige, and it smells like rubbing alcohol. Yeah, I am actually in the hospital. This sucks.

I need to find my phone so I can call my professors and let them know I am in the hospital. I also need my laptop to work on some homework while stuck in bed. In the world of law, cases don't handle themselves.

I hear the door open and look up. A tall older man with tan skin, salt and pepper hair, big blue eyes, and purple scrubs walks in. "Hello, Ms. Fayet, I am Dr. Price. I have been taking care of you all night. Mr. García told me your voice is hoarse, but I need to ask you some questions. I have one of my nurses getting you some water now. All I need is a thumbs up, middle, or down for answers." I look at him with concern on my face and try to squeak out more words. "I am…"

The nurse came rushing in with a paper cup with a bendy straw. I took the cup from her and took a small sip of water. Who knew water could be so delicious and comforting? The soothing cold water went down my throat, making me feel better than I did.

"I am sore in my stomach, my head hurts, I have a headache, and I can only recall a little bit of last night." I'm surprised I got all the words out without a single squeak this time. Everyone was staring at me like I had two heads. I'm not sure if it was because I spoke or what I said.

"What?" I ask, looking around the room.

"I wasn't expecting you to be able to speak with how hoarse your voice is." Dr. Price said.

Dr. Price and the nurse took my vitals, asked a series of questions, and then asked me to tell them what I knew about the night. They then went on their way, promising to check on me in an hour. Tucked away in the corner were the eyes I recognized from last night. It's one of the few things I do remember from last night. I keep looking at him, trying to figure out more of last night and how this man ended up with me at the hospital.

I sat there, staring at him for about five minutes before I gave up. I asked him, "Do you know what happened to me last night?" He looks up at me, and his face looks like that of a lost puppy dog.

"Um, yeah. You and a dude named Andrew got into an argument. My friend and I were driving by when he kicked you in the stomach, and you hit your head on a brick building. We stopped to help you and get Andrew contained so he couldn't hurt you anymore. You hit the back of your head pretty good; you needed some stitches, and you were bleeding all over the concrete. You asked me to come to the hospital so you wouldn't be alone." I nodded, soaking in everything he was saying, trying to get all the memories to return. Then, my hand goes to my stomach, and my mind goes to the baby.

"What about my baby? Did they say anything about my baby?" Disappointment is written on his face, and he replies, "Let me get the doctor or nurse so they can tell you about all of that. I am not sure of all of the terms and the doctor's talk." Once again, he is out the door. I probably should have asked his name before he left, so I could stop calling him Mr. García.

Not even five minutes later, an older female nurse came in. She was short, with grey hair and big-rimmed glasses hanging around her neck. Behind her was a tall, fit male doctor with beautiful, dark brown skin and the most beautiful golden brown eyes. "Hello, Ms. Fayet. My name is Tina. I am an OBGYN nurse, and this is Dr. Tyler. He is the doctor who took care of you last night."

"Hello, Ms. Fayet. As Tina said, I am Dr. Tyler. I did an ultrasound on you, and I am sorry to say that there was no heartbeat for your baby. I could also see the placenta starting to detach from your uterus. So, unfortunately, when you were in surgery, we had to do a D&C to remove the fetus before complications could happen to you. I am deeply sorry to bring you this terrible news. The baby passed due to the severe impact caused to your stomach yesterday from being kicked and when you hit the side of the building." Tears welled up in my eyes. I couldn't think straight, and it felt like my chest was tightening. No heartbeat? Miscarriage? D&C? Dead? This is all Andrew's fault!

"Thank you for... for trying to save my baby." My sobs made it almost impossible to talk to anyone right now. Tears run down my cheeks in huge drops, and I have snot everywhere.

"If you need anything, please let a nurse know. They can reach me, and I will be back immediately." I nod. Dr. Tyler hands me a box of tissues as he and Tina walk out the door.

I cried for an hour or more after Dr. Tyler left my room. My headache is worse than before, but that's the least of my concerns. I lost my baby! It wasn't because of developmental issues, and it wasn't because I messed up with what I ate or vitamins. This was all due to Andrew's temper. Maybe this is a sign that I wasn't meant to be a mom. Maybe this kid is better off without me as their mother. The tears keep streaming down my face as all the negative thoughts come rushing into my head.

I look up and see Mr. García sitting on the couch, hands on his lap, looking at the ground. I wipe my eyes and try to catch my breath to calm down enough to ask, "Hey, what's your name?" He looks up, confused that I was even talking to him. "Alejandro, but people usually just call me Alex."

Alejandro. I like that name. It rolls off the tongue. "Why are you here, Alejandro?" He looks at me kindly, but his eyes show only sorrow. You can tell he is scared to answer that question.

He finally nodded. "Please, just call me Alex. When the paramedics came to get you last night, you freaked out because you thought I wasn't going with you. You wouldn't let go of me once I told them I was going and grabbed your hand." That doesn't even sound like something I would normally do.

"Where is Andrew?" His face turned from soft and caring to rock-hard rage.

"He better fucking still be in jail!" He said through clenched teeth, as his fist balled so tight his knuckles were white. Noted. He is mad at Andrew.

"He is my fiancé. I need to contact him to let him know I lost the baby." I look over at Alex and don't even recognize the man with that much anger.

"He is the fucking reason you're in the damn hospital! He is the reason you lost the baby! Do you really need to tell him that he succeeded? That he got exactly what he wanted?" You can see his tan complexion turn red as he screams, hands flaring in the air. I shook my head as the tears ran down my cheeks.

"No, he wouldn't! He loves me. Sometimes, he drinks too much and escalates stuff, but I usually deserve it. I am not always tidy and don't always have food prepared when he gets home. I get frustrated and raise my voice. I deserve what he gives me." Tears are streaming down my face even harder now, and I start to hiccup.

"Losing the baby was my fault. I don't deserve this baby. It would be better off with a different mom. That's why my baby is gone." I screamed at him. All the pent-up grief came rushing out of me. I know I'm letting it out on the wrong person, but who knows when I would have completely lost it if it hadn't come out now? I am already teetering on the edge of sanity.

My baby is gone.

I could have protected the baby better. I shouldn't have pissed off Andrew. My baby would still be here if I had just waited to tell him. I was only twelve weeks pregnant, and my heart had a gigantic hole in it where the love for my baby is. This baby was already my whole life.

He rushes over to me, grabs my head, and starts to stroke my hair. "The baby getting killed was not your fault. Don't you dare for a second think that." All I could do in response was cry. I cried so much that I soaked through Alex's shirt with my tears and snot. My head is pounding again, and I feel like I might puke.

"Also, you won't be able to reach Andrew. The police put a restraining order in place last night, and he is in jail waiting for his trial." Alex said softly, trying to give me the news as gently as possible.

Oh no, no, no. This isn't good. He is going to be mad at me when he gets out. I'm going to get beaten for this. I need to figure out how to bail him out so he isn't stuck there. Maybe if I get him out, he won't blame me.

"I see those wheels turning in that pretty head of yours. Don't you dare try to bail him out! He did this to you!" I can feel the blood pounding in my ears; my heart is thudding in my chest. My hands are shaking and clammy, and my feet are tingling. This isn't good. My vision starts to blur, and it feels like I can't get any air into my lungs. Andrew is in jail, my baby is dead, and I am in a fucking hospital.

I can't get a full breath in my lungs.

I can't breathe.

I feel like I am suffocating.

"Hey! Hey hey hey." I can hear his words, but they sound funny, like I am underwater and sinking deeper.

"It's ok, we will figure this out. I won't let him hurt you again." I can barely hear his voice now; I am sinking deeper and deeper until all I hear is beeping in the background. Then everything fades out, and I am left with nothing but dark silence.

Chapter Seven

Alex

I let go of Rachel's hand and ran out the door to the
nurse's desk. "Something is wrong! She was breathing
funny and then blacked out! I hit the button, and no one
is coming fast enough! Someone do something!" I was
pacing next to the desk while a nurse paged someone to
the room. "Someone will be coming to the room, sir."
That was all she said, with a small smile. A fucking
smile! Like nothing is wrong, and that Rachel didn't just
pass out.

I run back into the room to be there when the doctor
arrives. She is still breathing, but she is out cold. I grab
her hand and wait as patiently as I can. Patients have
not been a strong suit in my life. My phone vibrates in
my pocket. I pull it out and see a text from Smith.

SMITH: Hey, I am out of Jail. Can you pick me
up? I am hungover as shit.

What should I say to him? I'm sorry, but I can't because I am with a girl I just met at the hospital. He is going to think I have completely lost my mind. I put my phone away and thought about this for a few minutes. The doctor finally came in; I will reply to Xander after they make sure Rachel is okay.

"Can you explain to me what happened?" I assumed the doctor was checking for a pulse when he started feeling around Rachel's neck. Still, I am not a doctor, so I have no idea what he is doing.

"Yeah, she started talking about the man who did this to her, Andrew, saying how he will be mad that he is in jail and that she needs to call him and bail him out of jail. Then she started to breathe heavily, and her body started to shake. I tried to calm her down, and then she passed out." The doctor nods to me in understanding, looks at the nurse, and says, "Just a panic attack." I can feel myself let go of the breath I didn't know I was holding. They don't seem to be freaking out, so I need to calm down. I pull out my phone to text Smith back, distracting my mind for a second.

> ME: Hey, man, you are going to have to get an Uber. I am at the hospital with a girl I rescued last night. Her "fiance" beat the shit out of her and kicked her into a building.

I don't care what he says. I am not leaving her; she asked me to be here for her, and I will be.

I wake up to someone gently running their fingers through my hair. I didn't even realize I fell asleep. I looked up and saw Rachel staring at me.

"Why are you staying here with me?" She whispers. I am still half asleep, but I sit up, stretch, and smile. "You asked me to stay here." Her lip turns up slightly, but you can see how sad she is.

"How are you feeling, Rachel?" I don't need her over-doing it and passing out again. "I'm OK, sore but better than I was yesterday." She gives me another one of her half-smiles. That is one of the cutest smiles I have ever seen... Also, the fact that she can smile after all that she has been through is crazy.

"Have you talked to the doctor about when I can get out of this shit hole?" She looks at me with so much hope in her eyes. "Yeah, they said you should be good to leave tonight as long as you stay stable and have no more panic attacks." Embarrassment washed over her face. "I hate that you had to see that. It's so embarrassing." She can't be serious right now... embarrassed? Over a panic attack? I look at her sternly and begin to say, "You don't have to be emb..." We get interrupted by a knock on the door. We look at the door, and Olivia pokes her head into the room. "Ms. Fayet, I am Officer O'Connor. I have a few questions for you. I was with Alex García the night we found you."

My heart is pounding. There is no way she is here, in the hospital. "Hey, Olivia, did you get assigned this case?" I asked. She shook her head and smiled shyly.

"No, I am involved personally, so I cannot take on the case. However, Officer Bennett has the case, and I have questions for Ms. Fayet regarding the incident for my own purposes. I will be on trial against Andrew when the time comes." I look over at Rachel; her eyes are tearing up, and you can hear her breath catch in her throat.

"I would love to help you, but my memory is foggy from that night." She looks around the room, noticeably uncomfortable.

"That is no problem, Ms. Fayet. I understand completely. We don't want to intrude. We just need a statement, but that can happen when you are ready and have time to recall what you can," Officer Bennett says in a gentle, soothing voice.

Olivia turned and smiled at me. "May I speak to you in the hall?" I look down at Rachel, who nods at me. I get up and follow Olivia out of the room.

"Hey, how are you?" I say. She turned around to look at me. "I have been better. How are you?" I looked at her, trying to figure out what was wrong.

"What's going on, Livy?" She looked at me, shocked when I called her by a nickname instead of her real name.

"It's just been crazy since I got back to work, trying to get this case handled without having my hands in it, and I just got a gang case dropped on my desk today. They want me to be the lead officer for the case." She looks excited but nervous at the same time.

"That's fucking awesome! Congratulations! I don't know much about the police force, but that sounds like a huge deal! I'm excited for you!" She gave a soft chuckle and mumbled her thanks.

Looking up at me, I said, "I wanted to give you my number so we can hang out again if you want to. We didn't get a chance for any of that after the incident." I smile at her, switch phones, and enter each other's numbers.

When I get back into the room, I see Rachel's face with tears running down her cheeks, and she is still talking to Officer Bennett. On the other side of the bed, the nurses are messing with some of the tubes that are attached to her. I'm not sure what they're doing, and I don't want to be in the way, so I sit in my chair, as far away from everyone as possible, and zone out.

"Mr. García, can I have a minute of your time to get a statement from you, too? I know you have been asked a lot of questions, but unfortunately, I have to ask more, " the officer says. I look over at Rachel, who is now chatting with the nurse and nodding at something she said.

"Yeah, no problem. Whatever I can do to help." She pulls me out into the hallway to talk. Why she couldn't just do this when I was already out in the hallway, the world may never know.

"So tell me, Mr. García. What do you recall from the night Ms. Fayet got attacked?" she asks me, and I give her a play-by-play of what happened. "So you were out with Officer O'Connor?" she asks judgmentally. I schooled my features so she wouldn't know that her question caught me off guard.

"Um. Yes. I asked her out on a date that night. What does that have to do with the case?" I ask with a side-eye. I am trying not to snap at this girl, but that's none of her damn business. "Thank you, Mr. García. Would you say you and Officer O'Connor are in a relationship?" She then bats her eyes at me like she is trying to be cute. "I apologize, Officer... um." I forgot her name. "Bennett. Officer Bennett." She replies with an eye roll and more sass than I have seen in a teenage girl. "Yes, Officer Bennett. No offense, but if Officer O'Connor and I are in a relationship, that is none of your concern. It is also completely irrelevant to the case and should not be asked right now," I say. She looked at me, her face heated with embarrassment.

"Right. Well, that will be all I need, Mr. García. Thank you for your time." With a nod, I walk back into Rachel's room and sit in my chair. She is on her laptop, completely focused on whatever she is doing.

"What are you studying?" I ask with curiosity in my eyes. She looks up at me, shocked, like I said the most ridiculous thing ever.

"Um. Law." She said, shocked I was even asking.

"Wow! Law isn't an easy major. You want to become a hotshot Lawyer when you are done?" I ask jokingly.

"I want to be a criminal defense Lawyer. I want to help those who were wrongly accused." Her eyes sparkle with care.

"I love the passion I can see in your heart. I know you will do great things in the field." I say and absolutely mean it. She just smiles at me.

"When do you graduate?" I say.

"Spring! I can't wait! I am going to apply to some smaller law firms soon to get my foot in the door. Then, I want to open my own Law firm." She speaks so fast, and her arms are flying in the air. You can feel the excitement radiating off of her.

After Rachel had studied for a while, she fell back asleep. It's likely because of the pain meds they have her on.

I am grateful she isn't a complete mess from the loss of the baby. I wouldn't know how to handle the situation if I were in her shoes, but I know I wouldn't be this strong.

I grab her phone and enter my number, just in case she needs me. I know she doesn't know me, but I will do anything to protect her. I'm not sure where these feelings are coming from, but they're hitting me like a semi-truck to the gut.

Chapter Eight

Rachel

Finally, I was out of the hospital and back in my bed. I am grateful that Alex stays with me and drops me off at home. He made it better, even though the whole time I felt numb.

I haven't done much after getting home besides checking the mail. I lay in my bed, trying to recover and zone out, thinking about everything and nothing at all. My brain doesn't know if it wants to shut off or not. My body hurts, and I don't know how to function like a normal human. I am on autopilot most of the time.

I finished my last semester at Yale. Thank god my professors let me do my work online since I was hospitalized, or else I would have been behind and not graduating in the spring. Now, I need to take time to focus on finding a job. But I have no motivation to do anything right now. I know as soon as I don't have school or a job, Andrew will be pissed.

Opening my laptop, I searched for Lawyer positions in San Diego. I uploaded my cover letter and resume to 3 different law firms. They are small, just like I wanted for my first job. Let's hope we hear back, but I am not getting my hopes up since I don't have my degree yet. I don't walk the stage until the end of next month. I made sure I finished classes early to try and get a job as soon as possible to avoid Andrew as much as possible. I am desperate not to be around him after everything that has happened. My mind still hasn't processed the fact that he kicked me into a wall. I mean, he has hit me before, and I know I deserved it, but to kick me seems a little extreme, and I can't figure out what I did wrong.

I am lost in thought, wondering if Andrew can post bail or not, what my baby would have looked like, if I should inspect the clots to see if I can see the baby's face at all, and what I would have been like as a mom.

My body and mind go numb again when the front door slams open, shaking the whole house. I am surprised the books on my shelf didn't fall. I look up to see Andrew storming into the house, growling as he rips the door from the wall, leaving behind a hole I will eventually have to patch up. I swear he will never learn to handle his temper; he just fucking growled at a door.

"Why are you just sitting on your fat ass? I swear you are a lazy sack of shit!" He yells while storming in my direction.

"I-I'm supposed to stay in bed as much as possible because of my injuries. I am also applying for jobs."

He rolled his eyes at me and snarled, "Quit being a lazy ass and get up! It's dinner time, and I am starving. What are you planning on cooking?"

" I can't, Andrew, I... I just ca..." I don't get to finish my sentence when I feel the sting on my cheek.

"You worthless waste of space! You can't even make a baby right! Now you won't cook dinner to keep your fiancé alive? What can you do?" He turns around and storms off towards the dining room table, pulling out his phone, reading something on it, and slamming it down onto the table. I won't be surprised if the screen is shattered.

I ignore his question as I roll out of bed, holding my stomach. That is where the most pain is. I am not sure if it is the miscarriage or the broken rib, but it fucking hurts. I head to the pantry and pull out some noodles and pasta sauce to make spaghetti. Quick and easy. As the water is heating to a boil, I go to the medicine cabinet to find the painkillers the doctors prescribed for me. I dig through the cabinet, and they are nowhere in sight.

"Hey, Andrew, have you seen my prescriptions from the hospital?"

He doesn't even look up from his phone. "Nope"

I don't believe him, but I just leave it be so I don't start an argument. He had been drunk and high a lot before he got locked up. He probably stole them as soon as he got home from jail so he could pass them out for money later this week. I guess I'll take some ibuprofen and call it good. Hopefully, this will make a change in the pain.

When the water is finally boiling, I add the noodles and wipe down the counters in the kitchen. I can feel the pain increasing so much that it is radiating up my back. I lean over the sink and vomit up all the contents of my stomach, which is water and stomach acid, because I haven't been able to eat. The pain of throwing up was excruciating. I get dizzy and collapse on the floor. I scream out in pain and grab my stomach. The room is spinning; I feel like my stomach is being ripped open. I need to get up to at least go to the bathroom in case I puke again.

"Get the fuck up off the floor! Why are you screaming? God! I swear, I can't believe I am even still with you. You're lucky I fucking love you! All you do is bitch and moan."

I slowly get back up to check the noodles and heat the sauce. The pain is still there, but Andrew is right; I should still be able to do things with some pain.

Once the pasta is done, I serve Andrew a plate and then head to the fridge to grab him a beer. He is on his phone, completely ignoring me. It's a typical night in our house. As I turn to walk back to the room, Andrew stands and charges towards me. Once in the bedroom, he grabs my wrists and pulls me toward him. I feel a pop in my wrist, and the bruising is already happening.

"Rachel!"

"Ow. Andrew, can you let go of me? You are hurting me."

He loosens his grip on me slightly. "If you would do what you were told, this wouldn't be an issue. Seriously, why can't you just follow simple instructions?" He looks down at me, his green eyes struggling to look as soft as possible, like he just gave me the best advice in the world.

He then wraps me in a hug, "Hey, Rae, I love you. I mean it, babe."

"I love you too," I say with a sigh as I rest in his arms, trying to stop being so scared.

He jerks my head up and smashes his mouth to mine, causing our teeth to hit hard. He starts to pull up my shirt...

"Please don't, Andrew. I don't want to have sex today. I am still sore, and I am not supposed to have sex after the surgery for at least a week. And I am still bleeding."

"A little blood has never stopped me before."

He rips my shirt down the center, and then my brand new bra I just bought. Next, he pulled at my sweats and snapped the elastic. Well, those are trash also now. He rips my panties off and pulls his cock out. He is already hard and strokes his shaft.

"Andrew, please don..." That was all I could get out before he slammed into me. I screamed out in pain. I have no time to adjust when he pulls out and slams in again. I am so sore, and his brutal thrusts are causing me excruciating pain. He continues to thrust harder and harder, each time significantly more painful, as he grunts in my ear.

I shut my eyes to picture myself somewhere else, any-where else but here.

Andrew finally finishes with one last final thrust and stills, falling on me once he is done. He pats my shoulder as if saying good game and pulls out. Getting up and heading straight to the bathroom.

I heard the shower turn on. I lay there on the floor, blood everywhere. My stomach felt like it was being ripped out of me, and I had cum dripping out of me. I feel like the whore Andrew claimed I was. I try to stand up. I grab the chair closest to me, pull up, lose my grip, fall, and hit my head on the table. I curl into a ball and just lie there until the pain subsides enough to get myself up and into bed.

Chapter Nine

Olivia

It's finally Saturday, and I am off work. The station has been in nonstop chaos. I am working with the gang unit to get intel about the Los Comos, also known as the Cali Cartel. We have been searching for anything for as long as I have been with the SDPD, and have always come up empty-handed.

I must remember that I am not at work and stop thinking about work. It's just so hard when my mind has been on "Las Comos" the whole week and nothing else.

As I look around my studio apartment, the TV is next to the door, with the bed and the kitchen to the right. The balcony is to the left. This is the ultimate bachelorette pad. I don't need much when I spend most of my time at the station.

I pulled out my phone and thought about Alex. I wondered what he was up to this weekend.

Me: Hey, it's Livy. What are you up to tonight?
I was thinking about maybe going out for a
beer.

After waiting an hour, I decided to go to the bar anyway. I'd have one beer, then return home to sleep away
my weekend. I pulled up my Uber app and ended up
at Hooligans, a bar closer to the Naval base. It's small,
but it sometimes has a live band. Tonight, it's Karaoke,
apparently. I won't be caught dead doing karaoke; I don't
like singing in front of people, even though Mama says I
have a great voice. I feel like that is what every mother
says to their kids.

Up at the bar, I am looking around at all the people.
None of them are my type, but the bartender is cute. He
is tall, with blonde hair, dark green eyes, and dimples!
He turns around to take the other customer's order. He
catches me eyeing him, and he winks at me. Man, it's
getting hot in here. I know my face has to be beet red.
He walks back up to me with all the confidence in the
world.

"What can I get for you, Beautiful?"

"Just a Budweiser, please."

"Wow, I wouldn't have pegged you for a Bud girl." I
don't know what he means by that, so I shrug and grab
the beer he set on the bar top.

"It's the only beer I will drink; my dad used to drink them with me while we would work on his project cars in the garage."

"Hmm, well, do you plan on staying here long tonight? I get off at 1 tonight. Maybe we can hang out after my shift." He smiles at me again with that panty-dropping smile and those damn dimples that will bring anyone to their knees.

"Yeah, I plan to sit here and watch the game." I tilt my chin toward the hockey game on the other side of the bar.

"So, which one are you going for? Chicago or LA?"

"The Vortex is my team. I have family from Chicago."

"Nice. Well, I had better get back to the other customers before they start jumping over the bar to get their drinks themselves." I chuckle and turn back to the TV, watching the game and drinking my beer.

I pull out my phone to see if Alex has read my message, and weirdly enough, it doesn't even look like it has been sent. His phone must be off, but I wonder why.

When I look back at the bartender, he winks at me and continues to help the customers lining the bar.

Once the bar dies down, he comes back my way and leans in to talk to me. "So Beautiful, what's your name?"

A smile plays on my lips. "Olivia."

"Hmmm, a beautiful name for a beautiful girl! I'm Mason."

"Do you want to go to the 24-hour Diner after you get off work? We could hang out and chat the morning away."

"Yeah, that sounds great, gorgeous. I will be thinking about that for the rest of the night. Hopefully, make this shift go by faster." He winks at me and then goes to help another customer who just came up to the bar.

Once Mason finally got off work, it was 2 a.m. The bar got busy, so he couldn't leave as planned at 1, so I sat there drinking and watching the games. Thank God I took an Uber here, because I wouldn't have been able to drive myself. Mason turned, coming out from the back hallway, where the staff area and bathrooms are, with the biggest smile on his face.

"Ready to go, beautiful?" I giggle and nod. Fuck I am more drunk than I thought, I don't giggle. Mason took my hand and led me outside to an old, black 1980 Chevrolet K10 square body. It looks like it has been taken care of, except for some minor dings that are to be expected with the truck's age.

Five minutes later, we pulled up to a small brick building that looked like it should have been shut down centuries ago. Vines were growing on the side of the building. Mason put his truck in park right in front of the building. He turned and looked at me. "Home sweet home, I guess." He seemed shy about it. Maybe embarrassed, I had no room to talk, because my house wasn't great either.

"Well, are you going to show me in or what?" I say in a flirty voice and wink at him. He undoes his seatbelt, walks around the truck to my side, opens the door for me, and reaches a hand out for me to grab.

Such a gentleman. "Thank you," I say as I take his hand and get out of the truck. As we walk up the stairs to his top-floor apartment, I listen to all the sounds around me. I hear some screaming from couples fighting about money, some guys talking about how high they are, and also some people fucking. It seems these apartments have no privacy.

We make it to the top floor, and Mason takes out his keys to open the door. When it swings open, it's surprisingly better-looking than the rest of the building. You can tell that Mason has put a lot of work into this apartment. "I own the whole complex. I bought it from the owner about a year ago, so I am trying to get it fixed up as best as I can. It's hard to do the apartments with tenants, so I do them as they move out before I rent them out again. Then I plan to work on the outside in between." He walks me into the apartment toward the kitchen. I stand back and appreciate the work he has done throughout his apartment.

"It looks nice in here. I can't wait to see what happens to the place when you get a chance to fix it all. I know you can make it look amazing." He chuckles slightly like he doesn't believe me and that he feels like only crackheads are going to live here forever.

"You want something to drink?" He asked, looking into the fridge. "I have beer, wine, water, juice, pretty much anything." He grabs a beer for himself while he waits for my answer.

"Beer is fine. Thank you." I start walking around and looking at the pictures on the walls. I assume these pictures are of his family. Seeing a bachelor with so many pictures on the walls is strange. I don't even have photos on my walls. I always thought I would move out of the apartment soon after I got it, so what's the point in decorating?

Mason approaches me, hands me the beer, and gestures for me to sit on the couch. I sit on the opposite side of him and sip my drink. Letting the awkward silence settle between us.

"So, how long have you been working at the bar?" I try to break the awkward silence.

He looks up at me with a glimmer of lust in his eyes. "Is this really what you want to talk about?" He asked with a chuckle.

"Well, no. Not really. But I was trying to kill the awkward silence." I admitted, turning towards him. We came here for one reason: drinking beer and asking about our day was not the reason.

After what feels like the longest thirty seconds, I look at him.

"So, are we doing this or what?" His eyes went big, and his jaw dropped with shock at how blunt I was.

"Oh, we are doing this!" he says in a deep, husky voice that sends a tingle of excitement straight through my body. He stands up and walks toward me like a tiger, ready to pounce on its prey. I am watching his every move as he gets closer to me.

He scoops me into his arms like I weigh nothing and walks me to the bedroom at the back of the apartment. Kicking open the door, he throws me on the bed and takes off his shirt. His green eyes sparkle with mischief.

"Strip!" he says to me with a dominant demeanor. I am not usually one to submit, but I guess I can make an exception tonight. I slowly get off the bed and seductively take off my clothes. When I am down to my matching emerald-green lace lingerie set, I sit back on the bed and look at Mason.

He climbs up on the bed, bends down, and kisses me, deep and hard. I feel his hands roaming around my body as mine do the same to his. He pulls back from the kiss, grabs my thong, and pulls it down my legs. Admiring me the whole time.

"Spread yourself open for me. Let me see my feast," he demands. Watching my every move as if he were memorizing it.

I slowly run my fingers down my chest and stop at my breasts to give them a gentle squeeze. Sliding further down my stomach to my thighs and back up to my wet pussy. Using both hands, I spread myself open to show Mason every part of me. He licks his lips as hunger burns in his eyes. I can see that he is barely holding onto his self-control.

I continue to play with myself, dipping my middle finger into my wet heat with one hand and grabbing my breast with the other, playing with myself as Mason watches from the side of the bed.

Finally, he breaks and dives headfirst into my pussy, rubbing his nose from my ass up to my clit, licking as he goes. The sensation causes me to arch my back and let out a breathy moan. He gets to my clit, nibbling and licking so much it is causing my breathing to pick up.

"Oh yes, right there. Please don't stop." I moan and scream out.

"Wouldn't dream of it, beautiful," he says, then dives back in.

Before too long, I was at the edge of beautiful bliss. Mason finally plunges his finger into my pussy, hitting that perfect spot, and I am free-falling into my orgasm.

Mason lifts his head and makes a show of wiping my release off his face and licking his fingers clean.

"That was intense," I say through ragged breaths. He finally takes off his boxer briefs and gives me that dimpled smile.

"Oh, baby, we are just getting started." He promises as he reaches the bedside table and grabs some condoms. I look at him with wide eyes.

"We have company coming over? Because that's quite a few condoms you have there, mister." I joke with him. I don't know if he is cocky and can actually perform that many times.

"Oh no, baby, these are all for you." Winking as he rips a condom from the bundle and throws the rest up by my head.

"Hold on tight, baby girl. This ride is just about to start." He says with a cocky grin and rips the condom open with his teeth and sheaths himself.

Without any warning, he thrusts forward all the way to the hilt, and I let out a scream. I had no time to adjust and wasn't prepared. He gives me a second to adjust, then starts to move.

He is slow and steady at first, but after a few thrusts, his tempo picks up, and his moves become animalistic. I have never had sex like this, but I am here for it. All I wanted tonight was a quick fuck, then to go about my day. Mason understood the assignment.

I am climbing the peak to my second orgasm, and I can feel that he is getting close to finishing, too. He reaches down and starts to rub my clit in circles with just the right pressure, and I combust.

"ALLLLEEEEEXXXXX," I yell as I orgasm, and then my hand flies to my mouth. Did I really just scream the wrong man's name in bed? Why the fuck would I scream Alex's name? What the fuck.

Mason freezes, and the look on his face can only be described as a mixture of confusion and pissed off. He pulls out of me and asks," Who is Alex?" For a brief pause, "Actually, never mind. I don't care. Just get out." While pointing towards the door.

"Mason, I am so sorry. I uh..." I try to explain to him what happened, but I don't have a real excuse.

"I said get the fuck out!" He yells.

I get off the bed, put on my clothes, and leave without a second glance. I pull up my Uber app to request a ride as I walk down the stairs to the lobby.

I am so embarrassed that I even did that. I have never said another man's name while I was in bed. Or women, for that matter.

Chapter Ten

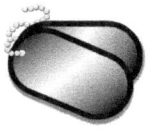

Alex

This Desert is hot as shit! I swear I have about five pounds of sweat in my boots, and I have no idea where we are going.

"Hey, Sir. Where are we supposed to be headed?"

"Up here, about five miles, is a small town we are stopping in."

"Yes, Sir."

Fuck, five more miles in this damn heat! I know I signed up for this, but damn, why can't we turn down the heat. Only the sun and sand are in sight for as far as I can see, and I could really use an ice-cold beer right about now. I know I am bitching about my own decisions.

I should have texted Olivia and Rachel to let them know I was leaving for at least six months. What am I even saying? Neither of them is my girlfriend, and I don't owe either of them an explanation. But fuck, the sound of them being my girlfriends is nice. How would that even work? Two women and me? That is every man's wet dream. I wonder if they are also into girls. That would make this dream even better! They are both hot; they would be even hotter together.

I get snapped out of my daydream by a loud explosion to the right of us. We duck down and cover our heads from shrapnel. Looking to the right, I see an MTV on its side engulfed in fire. Multiple people are groaning from the explosion, and honestly, a lot of body parts are landing on the ground.

"What the fuck!" Staff Sergeant yells.

"This is some minesweeper bullshit." Xander always makes a joke out of the situation.

"We need to watch our steps!" Our First Lieutenant says.

"Yes, Sir," we all say in unison. This man has been through everything we have been through. He has been with us every step of the way, taking us through the treacherous battles. Sometimes, I feel like the wars will never end. Whether it's in the Marines or with my grandfather, I will always be in some bullshit. At least with the Marines, I am doing something honorable for my country and not underground illegal shit.

Smith walks next to me and whistles the Don't Worry, Be Happy tune. It's ironic, given where we are and the explosion that just happened.

"What's up, dude?" I say to him with a side-eye.

"Nothing as crazy as that MTV over there." He says as he nudges me, and I roll my eyes.

"Dude. Too soon." I say back to him. I don't know how this man is always a half-full kind of guy. Like shit, he grew up as a military brat. His dad was in the Army, he knows firsthand how shitty this can be for a family, but yet here he is, always with a smile on his face and cracking jokes. I wish I could be as happy as that. I wish I could live in his mind for five minutes.

"Sooooooo, want to tell me about the night I got arrested?"

"Nope." I popped the P to emphasize my irritation about him getting arrested. My anger rises to the surface. I spin around and yell in his face.

"I have no idea why you had to swing first! If he had hit you first, he would have been the one behind bars!"

"I know. I was just mad that he was yelling at Ally, and then he pulled the Mexican card; you know how I feel about that shit. I don't know, I just... I saw red."

I shake my head. I understand, but it still is shitty. We had to talk to all the higher-ups about what we were doing, how it happened, and where I went after. It was stupid because some old fuck started it, and we got our asses handed to us.

I wipe off the sweat dripping down my forehead with the back of my hand and sigh at Smith. "I understand. It just fucking sucked. After you got taken to the station, I couldn't get the Officer out of my head. So, my dumb ass took an Uber to the station to wait for her to get off work...."

The dumbfounded look on Xander's face says it all!

"Wait! You waited outside the station for the cop who arrested me?"

I can't help the small smile that creeps up on my face. It happens every time I think of Olivia. Or Rachel, for that matter. To play it off, I roll my eyes, "Did I fucking stutter? I know I have an accent and shit, but you have never had a problem hearing me before."

Xander shakes his head and rolls his eyes. "You know what I mean, jackass! Was she at least good in bed?"

I shook my head and shrugged at the same time. "I don't know. We didn't make it to bed. We ended up at the diner, had a nice chat, then she was driving me home, and we saw some dumb ass kick a woman in the stomach into a brick wall. So I got out to help her. She wanted me to go to the hospital with her, so Olivia took care of Andrew, and I took care of Rachel."

We finally walked up to a clearing. Sir is telling everyone where to set up camp. We are about three miles outside of the village. Enough space to not be in the way, but also to be able to make it there in time if shit hits the fan.

Xander and I are setting up the tent when he finally mentions anything about the situation I just told him about.

"So, do you know why the asshole kicked the chick?"

"She said he got mad because she told him she was pregnant." I quietly stated while looking around. It's really no one's business what happened to Rachel.

"I stayed with her in the hospital for three days while she recovered; she had to have surgery because of a bunch of different internal things, but they also had to do a thing called a D&C to remove the baby from the uterus because it didn't make it through the impact. She had a broken rib, concussion, and some internal bleeding."

"Holy fuck!" Xander said with eyes reaching his brows.

"Yeah. It wasn't good. The weird thing also is that when we went to the hospital, she had no next of kin, so I was designated to make all the medical decisions for her because the paramedics heard her freaking out when she thought I wasn't going with her to the hospital."

"Holy shit! Is that even legal?" The shock in his voice is prominent.

"I asked the nurse the same thing. They said since she knows me, sorta, I guess, and she had no next of kin, I was put as her responsible person for any medical decision." This conversation flows while we feel like dying in the desert from the heat and sun.

"That's intense, man. So, did you even get to know her at all while in the hospital?" Damn, this dude is so nosey, but I guess it's for good reason. I haven't been in a real relationship for almost three years now.

"You are telling me. But, yeah, we got to know each other while at the hospital. But before you ask, no, not in a sexual way! She just lost her baby. I am not that kind of man." I sighed and wiped the sweat off my face. It was a crazy ass couple of days. "And to think, the fucker got out on bail also. I swear to god, if he hurts her again, I'm going to kill him. And I will make him suffer miserably."

It all came out before I could stop what I was saying, and Smith caught on right away.

"Oh really? You already caught the feels?" He says with a mischievous glint in his eyes.

"Enough about me! What's been going on with you? Haven't heard from you much lately." I try to change the subject to anything besides my confusing as fuck thoughts about Rachel, and let's not bring up Olivia. These two women are a topic I am not ready to dissect.

"Nothing much. I went back home for a couple of days before we left. Went to see mom and get some home cooking before we got here and ate only shit." He mentions. But I can tell he is hiding something because he is not looking at me.

"Is that it? You aren't going to tell me about all the pussy you got while at home. Don't you usually have a line of women waiting for you when you get home?" He is a playboy, and we're aware of it.

I raise an eyebrow at him when he doesn't answer me.

"Got it. Don't want to talk about it." I say while chuckling. "How's Mom?" I ask. That lady is a lifesaver. She has taken me in just as much as my mom has taken Xander in. It must be the single-mom thing.

"She is good." He said simply. Something is going on, but I won't push it right now.

Once we set up camp, we made our way to the little town. It felt like the sun had beaten us down for a hundred hours. This town has about ten little huts, children running around in what looks like rags, and parents doing various work. The outside perimeter has makeshift barriers with logs, nails, and barbed wire.

I wonder how many people live here.... As I look around again, I see a little girl with big brown doe eyes and long brown hair on the bottom of her back that looks like it hasn't been washed or brushed in years, and a dress that honestly looks like it is made from a burlap sack, running up to me. She seems too innocent to be put into a position like this. None of the children should have to worry about a war being waged in their own home.

The look on the little girl's face was pure joy when I smiled and waved to her. I kneel down in front of her and reach into my cargo pocket. I pull out a small top and spin it on the ground for her. Her eyes light up like the 4th of July. Once it stops spinning, I pick it up and hand it to her, and she runs off with it, yelling something I don't understand. She shows the other kids, and they all look at it in amazement. I walk up to the group of kids and hand out the remainder in my pocket so they can all play with them. They all nod at me to say thank you and run around spinning tops everywhere.

I will have to ask Ma to get these kids more Dollar Tree toys. I will also ask her to send me some Tide Powder so the families can wash their clothes and other items, which would simplify their lives just a little bit. They are living through hell right now, and I am pretty sure we are here to protect this little village, even before it's confirmed.

"We are heading back to camp," Sir yells out.

"Yes, Sir." We all say in unison as we grab our packs and start getting all our stuff ready to return to camp.

When we returned, I looked around to see what I could do to make this camp a little more homey, but I found nothing. I finally gave up and sat down. I pulled out my notebook and started writing. Because of Rachel and Olivia, I had so much on my mind; I just needed to get it out.

HEY RACHEL,

I AM OVERSEAS, BUT YOU WOULDN'T KNOW THAT BE-CAUSE I DIDN'T TELL ANYONE BECAUSE I AM A DUMB ASS. BUT I WISH I COULD SEE YOU AND KNOW YOU ARE HEALING. MAKE SURE ANDREW DOESN'T PUT HIS HANDS ON YOU AGAIN. I'M SORRY I WON'T BE THERE FOR YOUR GRADUATION, BUT I AM SUPER PROUD OF YOU, AND I ALSO KNOW YOU WILL BE THE MOST AMAZING DEFENSE LAWYER IN SAN DIEGO. GO GET THEM! PLEASE KEEP THAT BEAUTIFUL SMILE ON YOUR FACE AND KNOW YOU ARE AMAZING.

ALEX

I turned the page and started another letter. Knowing they will never be sent out to the people they are intended for allows me to write freely and open up about my feelings that I am confused about.

So, I will write about my absolutely ridiculous feelings in this notebook. Feelings that shouldn't be there because I barely know these women. But god, I would love to get to know them. I would love to learn everything about each of them. I also want to get to know every inch of them.

Olivia,

I KNOW YOU ARE PROBABLY PISSED OFF AT ME BECAUSE I DIDN'T MENTION WHERE I WAS GOING. I WANT TO SEE YOU AGAIN AS SOON AS I GET HOME. I WANT TO LEARN EVERYTHING ABOUT YOU. I'D LOVE TO HEAR ABOUT YOUR DAYS, DREAMS, AND AMBITIONS. I WANT TO HEAR ABOUT YOUR LIKES AND DISLIKES. I WANT TO KNOW EVERYTHING THAT MAKES YOU WHO YOU ARE. I DON'T KNOW WHERE THESE FEELINGS MUSTERED UP, BUT I FEEL LIKE I HAVE KNOWN YOU MY WHOLE LIFE, AND THAT YOU ARE SUPPOSED TO BE HERE FOR THE REST OF OUR LIVES. YOU FEEL LIKE HOME TO ME. I KNOW THIS MAKES NO SENSE, BUT I HAVE NOTHING BETTER TO DO IN THIS DESERT THAN THINK

Alex

These letters made me feel lighter and, honestly, giddy, like a little kid. I look to my right and see Smith, deep in thought, writing something in his own notebook. I look over, and I know the name Aria. I vaguely remember a girl named Aria from his hometown. I remember they were childhood best friends. I could ask him about her sometime and see what he says. But after the short replies he made earlier today, I am assuming the subject is off-limits.

Chapter Eleven

Rachel

It has been a month since the accident, and Andrew has returned to his usual self, working, coming home, eating dinner, playing games, and sleeping. He is usually high, drunk, or both when he walks through the door.

I will walk the stage at the end of this month, so I have been applying to as many law firms as possible. I just need to get my foot in the door, and then I will know all my hard work has been worth it.

I put away my laptop and grabbed my book to read and relax, but I heard the door slam open. Well, there goes any chance of me relaxing.

"Where the fuck are you, Rachel!" Andrew yells while stomping down the hall so hard that I'm surprised there aren't cracks in the tile.

"In the room," I called back. I'm not in the mood for his temper today, so hopefully, if I can figure out what he needs, he will leave me alone.

As he walks into the bedroom, you can smell the whiskey on his breath; his eyes are bloodshot, and he bumps into the wall with every other step he takes.

"How much have you had to drink, Andrew? It's only eleven in the morning, and you are drunk!"

He stumbles up to me and grabs me by the throat, picking me up off my chair. I claw at his hand on my throat, but that only makes him squeeze tighter.

"Why don't you mind your own business, you fucking whore!"

Whore? What have I done? I have never been unfaithful to Andrew. I don't even go out with friends to bars because of the possibility of someone flirting with me and Andrew blaming me.

"What. Are.." I can't get any more words out. I can't get any air into my lungs.

He shakes me with the grip he has on my throat. "That fucking Beaner! The one that was with you in the hospital! Who is he?"

He loosens his grip a smidge so I can talk. I sucked in as much air as I could get into my lungs. "Alex? He is just a friend who made sure I was ok during my stay at the hospital. There was nothing more that happened."

I swear, I saw Andrews's eyes shift, and the next thing you know, my head was flying towards the wall! Andrew then pulls me back to his face, so close he is spitting on me, "You fucking lying bitch! You fucked him! Didn't you?" Slamming my head into the wall again. Spots dance around in my vision, a headache is starting to form, blood is dripping down my forehead, and I am extremely dizzy.

Andrew throws me to the ground. I hit my head on the bed in the process of falling. " Didn't! You!" He emphasizes each word. When I looked up, I saw his foot coming toward my face. The only thing I could do before impact was close my eyes. The nasty sound of a crunch echoed out as his boot made contact.

"You. Fucking. Whore!" He screamed out, tapping my chest with each word and spraying spit all over my face. One of his hands is on his belt to undo it, ripping it through the belt loops, and then he pops the button off his pants and unzips them.

"You just don't know how good you have it! You get to go to school and not worry about bills or anything! Just get your little degree so your pride won't be hurt. Let me show you how fucking good you have it here. You spoiled bitch." He pulls down his pants, almost falling over in the process. He grabs hold of my desk for support, knocking over my books and laptop that are sitting on top. I scooch back and try to sit up. He swings and punches me in the side of the head, causing the dizziness to come back harder.

"Stay down bitch! I'm not done with you! You seriously couldn't just do what I asked of you. It's too hard... Poor Rachel can't get simple tasks done." He keeps taunting me. Bending down onto the floor now that he is bare from the waist down, he rips my legs apart.

He easily has a hundred pounds on me, but I continue fighting as best as I can with the pounding headache and aching throughout my body.

"Your fight makes me so hard. Keep fighting me, Rachel. Be the perfect little slut for me. I might have to do this more often. God, you are so perfect for me, Rach." He starts to pound into me at a brutal pace, every thrust hurting more than the one before. "Yes, Rach, right there!" He keeps saying dirty things to me as if it's supposed to make this any better and make me get into the mood. I block the pain and his words out of my mind. I think about the beach and the beautiful waves. Anything besides this version of Hell I am currently in.

Finally, with one final thrust, he grunts and starts to shudder. He leans over me, sweat dripping off his forehead onto my face, and I can feel his warmth filling the inside of me. He falls on top of me.

"Thank you, baby, for that. You are the best thing that has ever happened to me." He says before rolling to his side to get off of me.

What the fuck is wrong with this man. Is he delusional? He just said thank you to me for him raping me. I sit up slowly, trying to be as quiet as possible. I crawl towards my desk and get one of my old textbooks off the ground. Swinging it as hard as I could, I hit him on the head.

I stand up after I hit him and take one final look. He is visibly shaking, and his fists are clenched at his sides. A menacing smile appears as he looks from me to the wall, where a picture of us is hanging, taken during a hike. Fuck. I thought that would knock him out. I turned around to go out the door and realized he had locked it. I fumble with the lock, trying to unlock it, but my adrenaline is going too fast, and my hands can't keep up. When I finally get the lock unlatched, he grabs the picture and smashes it on my head, then grabs me by the back of the neck and throws me across the room.

"You stupid bitch! You think you are strong enough to hurt me? Just for that, I am going to fucking destroy you." Andrew is stalking towards me. I am holding my head, which is bleeding again, and I see a black tunneling my vision. This is it; Andrew is finally going to kill me.

Chapter Twelve

Olivia

We are slowly getting more evidence against Los Comos. It has been a lot of he said, she said with no solid evidence. Every lead we get somehow disappears. I know those fuckers are making them disappear, but the question is. How? I don't know which direction we have to go to get something solid on them.

On paper, they are as clean as a whistle, but everyone in San Diego is aware of them and knows they run the Cartel in Southern California. It's not a secret, so why is this so difficult?

I am sitting at my desk, searching for any information about current murders, money laundering, missing women or children, or anything to lead me in the right direction. My mind starts to drift off to Alex. I wonder why he hasn't texted me back. I wonder what he is doing. Why do I even care? I shouldn't care; he is the one who ghosted me. That's his problem, not mine. He missed out on what fun we could have had.

I am not conceited by any means, but I know I am not ugly, and he is beyond gorgeous; between his dark chocolate eyes, Marine Corps high and tight brown hair, his beautiful sun-kissed tan skin, and that panty-dropping smile with dimples that make me weak in the knees. I let my mind wander for a minute, allowing myself to think about everything that is Alex.

I pull out my phone to stalk his social media accounts. His last post was the Friday after our date. It is a picture of him in a black Henley shirt, wearing sunglasses and a backward baseball cap, with the sunset behind him, as he holds up a peace sign. The only thing that it says is "Peace Out." I wonder what the fuck that means. My mind is wandering all over the place. I am super curious about where he went. Why does it just say peace out? What does that mean? Why do I care?

I finished what little work I had left and logged out of my computer. I grabbed my jacket and walked out the door; I didn't have time to deal with any of my coworkers right now. They would ask me if I wanted to go to the bar or hang out, but all I wanted to do was lie on the couch in my fuzzy blanket and read a smutty book.

On my way home, I stopped at the little Chinese restaurant near my apartment. Of course, a smutty book always goes well with chow mein and orange chicken. While waiting for my food, I overheard a man on the phone who mentioned something about "the product being shipped" and Lopez García. My interest is piqued. I tried to listen more; there were mentions of the feds, bait, and a grandson. The man spoke extremely fast; some things were hard to pick up from this distance.

I want to listen more, but my order is up. I made sure to pin this knowledge and come back to it. I wonder what type of bait they are talking about. I will need to mention this to the guys. What if it's another woman they use as bait? Who are they baiting?

I decided to deal with this knowledge when I returned to the office. Right now, I need a good book, food, a shower, and sleep. That's the plan, and I am sticking to it.

When I get home with my takeout, I set the bag on the coffee table and get my bottle of wine from the fridge. It's been a day, and I plan to relax. I turn on the TV, put on some shitty romcom to fill in the quiet while I eat my food.

I started to take out my Chinese to-go containers, and my mouth started to water as soon as I pulled out the egg drop soup. I pop the lid off, put an unhealthy amount of black pepper on my soup, and dig in. This soup is my absolute favorite thing in this whole world. I would live off this soup if I could.

I zone out as I eat my food, and once again, my mind goes back to Alex. I think about the conversations we had at the Diner. The way his eyes shone as he was dancing like a crazy person in my passenger seat, and I also think about all the anger I saw on his face when he saw Andrew kick Rachel. The man may not admit it to anyone, but he wears his heart on his sleeve.

I pulled out my phone and saw that there were still no messages from him. I won't lie, I am a little butthurt that I'm getting ghosted. But I have to remember it's his loss. I trade out my phone for my book on the coffee table. I want to escape reality and enter a fantasy world. I need a morally grey man to distract my mind. An unhinged book boyfriend is always better than a real man.

Chapter Thirteen

Alex

6 Months later

October

We are finally on our way back home. This deployment was completely necessary for the life of the small village. Ensuring those families had a safe place to live and raise their children made every moment, every drop of sweat, and every sunburn worth it. It's stuff like this that makes me love what I do. This is why I signed up to be a Marine. It is never the same thing with each deployment. I am here to help people in this world full of chaos and destruction.

I would know all about the destruction coming from the Lopez García name. This is why people only know me as García. My grandfather is the head honcho of the

Cali Cartel. Yes, you heard that correctly... I am the heir to Los Comos since he only had my mom as a child, which makes me next in line. And I don't want it! I want nothing to do with the Cartel. Human trafficking is the part that gets me queasy. How could you be willing to sell a human being and sleep at night?

As I get off the plane with my pack slung over my shoulder, my aviators are on while the sun beats down the flight line. It's nice not to be in a thousand-degree weather.

Xander walks up next to me, putting on his Ray-Bans, and whistles "Shake It Off" by Taylor Swift. I am envious of his carefree personality. If I didn't come from the bloodline that I do, I would be able to be carefree, too. The problem is that my family is a part of the destruction going on, and while my grandfather is the Drug Lord, I have no power to help the innocent.

"Hey, man. You good?" Xander pulls me out of my head.

I hate it when I go down this rabbit hole. I need to get out of my head about my family issues and worry about my current life in the Marine Corps. Taking over the Cartel is an issue for another time.

"Yeah. Just a lot on my mind." I smile at him. Hopefully, it was convincing. I pull out my phone and turn it on. After six months of being gone, my phone was buzzing nonstop. I finally looked at it when everything had calmed down. I had over 100 text messages and 50 phone calls. I slowly scrolled through all of the text messages and froze!

Olivia: Hey, It's Livy. What are you up to tonight? I was thinking about maybe going out for a beer.

Holy shit! My jaw drops, and my heart rate picks up. I can't believe that, out of all the times a beautiful girl could have texted me, it was right after I left for deployment. She probably thinks I ghosted her. Hopefully, she got the impression that there was no way I would ever do such a thing to such a beauty. I quickly shot off a short message to her. Hopefully, she replies, and we can see where this goes. My hands are shaking as I am trying to type.

Me: Hey, It's Alex. I just got back stateside. If you would let me, I can explain more. If you allow me the honor, I would love to take you to dinner and explain.

Damn. I sound pussy whipped. When the fuck did I start saying, "If you would allow me the honor." I shake my head, not sure what has gotten into my confidence, but apparently it ran the fuck away.

I put my phone back into my pocket and walk to my bike. Xander and I parked our bikes next to the barracks so no one would fuck with them while we were gone. I finally got to my Black Harley-Davidson. This is my bitch! I love this bike more than anything else. I pull my leather jacket out of my pack and put it on, along with my helmet. I swing my leg over my bike and start it up. The purr of the engine fuels my soul. God, this bike is exactly what I need right now.

I slowly ride my bike through the streets of NBC, enjoying the freedom of riding again. Once I get off base, I let the wind take me wherever it wants. The world passes me by with the freedom of my bike under me. I love this feeling—the freedom. There are no responsibilities and no obligations—just me and my bike.

I ended up on the beach. I put up the kickstand and swung off the bike. I removed my helmet, placed it on the seat, and began walking down the boardwalk, breathing in the salty air and feeling the breeze through my hair. This is my happy place—the beach and my bike—and I can't wait to bring whoever I fall in love with here.

I feel my phone buzz when I finally sit on the bench to look out at the water. It's Olivia!

> Olivia: Hey, stranger! Long time no talk. Want to get pizza tonight?

> Me: Pizza sounds great. Want to go to the Filippi's?

> Olivia: Awesome! 6?

> Me: Perfect! See you then, beautiful!

I'm so giddy about this date. I haven't been this way since high school when I asked Kaylie Shay to prom, and she said yes. I should go home and get ready for this date with this beautiful lady.

I get home and throw my pack on my bed. I'll deal with that later. Heading into the bathroom, I turn on the shower and undress. You can see the tan lines from the rolled sleeves of my uniform and from spending too much time in the hot sun. I step into the shower and sigh in relief. You never know the small things you miss until you don't have access to them every day. The most amazing feeling in the world is when you haven't been able to take a decent shower in six months, and then you get to stand under the water, letting the water run down your body for ten minutes without moving. I probably should wash up and get ready for my date.

Standing in front of the mirror in my bathroom, I stare at my reflection while doing up the buttons on my red dress shirt. I can see some of the scars from my time overseas. Shrapnel got me from an explosion near our camp. That explosion, thankfully, didn't kill any of our people, only causing injuries, some more severe than others, but Doc was able to patch us up, and we kept going. Doc said my cuts were the deepest, and I had to get a couple of stitches, but that's all.

I have to shake my head to clear my thoughts of deployment. I don't need to be thinking about that before a date. I brush my teeth and spritz some cologne on my neck before heading down the stairs to get my helmet and bike keys. Now that I'm supposed to be home for a while, I should look into getting a new vehicle to have something other than my bike as my daily driver.

Chapter Fourteen

Olivia

I am still shocked that I got that text from Alex. I was sure he had forgotten about me. It has been six months since I texted him, and I haven't heard back. He said he just returned stateside, so I wonder what that means. I wonder if it was a deployment. I remember him mentioning he was a Marine that night at the diner. I guess I'll find out at dinner. He said he would explain, so I will make sure he does because it doesn't make sense to disappear without a word.

I get in the shower and wash up. I'm shaving everything so I am smooth in case anything happens tonight. I am not expecting it, but a girl can hope since the last time I had sex was with Mason, and that was six months ago when I made a complete fool of myself. After my shower, I put on natural-looking makeup and blow-dried my hair, taming this unruly mane.

Once I've finished everything in the bathroom, I make sure to throw my dirty clothes and towel in the hamper and head to my closet. What the fuck should I wear? It's just pizza, so I don't want to overdress, but I still want to impress him. I stare at my clothes for an hour before deciding on a cute black lace top and a pair of jeans. I top it off with my leather jacket and black, chunky, round-toed, high-heeled ankle boots. It's nothing too fancy. I got my heels on clearance for $10, but it was the best money I ever spent. These boots are my go-to for any occasion. I sit on the couch, buckle up my boots, and relax until it's time to go.

When 5:45 arrives, I get up from the couch, where I've been scrolling through social media, and head to the kitchen, where my purse and keys are. I live five minutes from the pizza restaurant, so I'm leaving now. I will still be early, but not too early. Being late makes me anxious, so I always make sure I am at least ten minutes early for any plans.

I walk in, and Alex is already at a table. My breath catches at how gorgeous this man is; those six months have done nothing but make him look even better. He waved me over with the biggest smile and stood to pull out my seat. Such a gentleman. *It's okay, Olivia. You can do this. This is not the first time you have been around a handsome man who has manners.*

I smile as I sit and mumble my thanks. "How have you been?"

"I have been okay. I just returned from deployment, so I didn't receive your text until today. I am sorry I didn't tell you before I left." Woah! This whole time I wondered where he was and why he wasn't replying. Why didn't I consider the possibility that he might be on deployment? I feel like a complete jackass for even thinking he ghosted me while he was out defending our country.

"How was your deployment? Where did you go? Can you even tell me?" I spew out. I can feel my cheeks heating up from embarrassment. I cover my face. "I'm so sorry. I just threw a lot at you."

He laughs. I didn't know I missed the deep rumble laugh until I heard it again. That is one of the most incredible sounds I have ever heard.

"Don't be sorry. I will answer as many of your questions as I can. The deployment wasn't too bad. It was extremely hot, but we were in a little village helping them rebuild and get their feet on the ground after getting run over by terrorists."

"WOW!" I damn near screamed in his face. "That's absolutely amazing."

"I swear I wasn't ghosting you. I know you didn't say that, but I can only imagine what you felt when you texted me, and I didn't reply for six months."

We ended up talking for hours about anything and everything. The conversation was so natural, it was the absolute best feeling. I haven't felt this carefree in a long time.

I look up from my glass with a smile at Alex. "Hey, would you like to go to my house and have another beer since the restaurant is about to close?"

His eyes shot up to his eyebrows, and he looked... nervous? I think.

"Uhhh. Yeah sure. That sounds great." Yeah, he is definitely nervous.

"Is that nervousness I hear in your voice, Mr. García?" I laugh and tease him.

He rolls his eyes and shrugs at me.

"We can't be perfect all the time. I will follow you to your place on my bike."

He drops two one-hundred-dollar bills on the table. He walked around the table and held out his hand for me.

"Such a gentleman," I chuckle as I grab his hand.

I pull into my parking spot at my apartment five minutes later. Alex follows, pulls his black motorcycle beside my car, and removes his helmet. Holy shit, I swear I felt my panties get wet just from the view of this man taking off his helmet. I had never thought a man on a motorcycle was so sexy until now. Now I'm questioning whether I need to get laid or if I've suddenly developed a thing for guys on motorcycles. I had to tell my pussy to calm down before I got out of my car and jumped his bones.

Okay, Olivia. You can do this. He is a very hot guy, but he's just a guy.

Okay, something is seriously wrong with me. I have never talked to myself so much until today. I also have never been this flustered sexually before.

I finally mustered enough courage to get out of the car, and Alex was leaning against his bike. I mentally have to tell my lady bits *"down, girl"* again. This man will cause me issues; whether it's good or bad is yet to be determined. Here goes nothing, or absolutely everything...

We walk up the stairs to my little apartment, and I fumble with my keys to get them into the lock. I am a nervous wreck. I am grateful that Alex hasn't commented on how shaky I am.

As soon as I get the door open, I turn to Alex and smile. "I know it's not much, but it's home."

The heat flickered in his eyes, and the next thing I knew, he shoved me up against the door, mouth over mine in a rough and needy kiss. All thoughts in my head vanish; all I can do is feel.

Feel his hands on my hips to pull me close.

Feel his lips on mine.

Feel his tongue battle mine for dominance of this kiss.

Feel the passion, want, and need.

I have never been able to live in the moment, but I could live in this moment for the rest of my life.

Chapter Fifteen

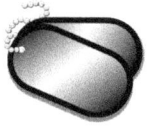

Alex

I probably should have taken things slower, but fuck it. It's not who I am; I am a go-big-or-go-home kind of guy. Walking up the stairs and watching her gorgeous ass swing from side to side made me hard as a rock. I had to adjust my pants multiple times just to get up the stairs to her apartment. Staying patient while she fumbled with the keys was hard. I could feel the nerves radiating out of every part of her. Once inside, she said something that sounded like, "This is home," but I was barely paying attention. I couldn't take it anymore. I shut the door with my foot, which caused it to slam a little louder than I intended, and pushed her up against the door. I kissed her as if my life depended on it. And, at that moment, my life, in fact, did depend on it. I needed to kiss her more than I needed my next breath.

A soft moan escaped her lips. I made sure to catch every sound she would give me with my mouth. I ran my tongue over the seam of her lips, seeking entrance, and as soon as I got the access I so desperately craved, our tongues swirled in the dance of need. She gripped my shirt with both of her hands and pulled me as close to her as we could possibly get with clothes on. I grabbed the base of her auburn hair and wrapped my hands in it. I give it a slight pull to see how she reacts to me, and I am rewarded with one of the sexiest moans I have ever heard in my life.

She pulls my shirt over my head and runs her hands down my chest and abs, feeling every inch. I grab her hair harder this time and slam my lips back to hers. I had to have that connection with her again. It was impossible not to want to taste her or feel her.

I finally released her, looking down into her beautiful blue-green eyes, rosy cheeks, and kiss-swollen lips. But I need to see all of her. I step back to admire all of her. A growl leaves my throat that is more animal-sounding than human. I need to see all of her. NOW!

I grab the hem of her shirt, slowly lift it over her head, throw it to the side, and reach for the button on her jeans. She grabs my pants, pulls me closer to her, and puts her mouth back on mine for a quick kiss as she frantically pops the button on my jeans.

She takes a step back, and we rush to remove our pants ourselves. I decided to take off my boxers; there was no point in keeping them on. I look up and see Olivia admiring me while standing in her red lace bra and matching thong. Her red hair cascaded down her chest and hung next to her beautiful breasts, all of her creamy pale skin on full display for me to indulge in. Her right arm has a tattooed sleeve; it looks like a landscape scene, with everything from trees, mountains, a stream, birds, deer, flowers, and butterflies. She is absolutely flawless. I can't wait to memorize every square inch of her body.

I reach for her, and she steps into my arms. I'm not sure why, but this specific movement felt oddly intimate. I reach around and unclasp her bra, slowly sliding it off her shoulders to release her gorgeous tits. If I had to guess, I would say she is a solid D cup with rosy, perky nipples begging for my mouth.

I grab her breasts in my hands and squeeze lightly, rolling the pebbled nipples in my fingers to get them more taut. I give her one more quick kiss before I lower my face to her breasts. Licking and swirling her nipple in my mouth while massaging the other. I switched to give the other side the same amount of attention. She throws her head back and grabs the back of my head to pull my head into her breasts more. If I suffocate right here, just know I died a happy man.

I look over to the bed and back at her, moving my head toward the bed to signal her to lie down. She does as she is told, but puts a little more sway in her step as she walks towards the bed. She slowly takes off her thong in a striptease.

"So beautiful," I admire from my spot near the door. Never in my life have I been so grateful for a studio apartment as I am right now. I only have to take five steps, and I am right in front of her. I reach down into my pants, pull out my wallet, grab the condom, and toss my wallet on top of the mess of clothes on the floor.

I finally get to the bed and set the condom on the nightstand while I look down and stare at my Azúcar and watch her squirm under my gaze.

"Are you going to sit there and stare at me like a hungry bear or actually take a bite?" She sasses with one eyebrow up as if she is challenging me.

"You are a brat! You know that, Azúcar?" She shrugs and bites her lip, looking me up and down with hunger in her eyes.

I get up onto the bed, sitting between her thighs. I lean down and kiss her deeply, moving from her lips to her neck, kissing and sucking, trying to mark my territory. I would be lying if I said I didn't want to leave hickeys all over her perfect body. Let the world know who she belongs to.

I drag my tongue down her collarbone, to the crease between her breasts, down her belly, until I get to her hip bone. I look up at her as I slowly go down to her little patch of hair shaped like a heart. I sit up to look at it better and raise an eyebrow at her. All I get in reply is a wink. I swear this girl is going to be my death.

I get back to work. Slowly licked from her puckered hole in the back until I hit the little bundle of nerves. I gently nip her clit before swirling my tongue around it to soothe the sting. She moans so loud I think the neighbors will hear her, but I couldn't care less. It brings the feral beast out in me, and I am about to claim what is mine. I lick and suck every inch of her pussy; she has the sweetest taste I have ever had on my tongue, which makes me eat her like a man who is starving to death.

I insert a finger into her warm tight cunt, hitting that perfect spot to cause her to squirm and buck under my touch. I slowly pump my finger in and out of her to match the rhythm of my tongue, causing her to get close to the edge. Her breath is getting faster, and she wiggles more under my touch.

"No, No, Azúcar. You won't be cumming on my fingers. I want to feel you milk my cock with your tight pussy. I want to feel your juices running down my balls."

Her eyes get big as she gasps and nods at me like that is exactly what she wants.

I smile at her as I lean over and grab the condom from the nightstand. Before I can sit back up, she snatches the condom out of my hand and gives me the most mischievous grin.

"No, allow me to sheath this beautiful cock."

She grabs my cock and strokes it a few times before leaning down and running her tongue up the base of my cock to the tip, swirling her tongue over the tip to gather the pre-cum. She hums in approval and swallows me whole, her eyes never leaving mine.

Coming up for air, she mutters, "Fuck you are so big, I'm not sure you will fit."

She pulls my dick out of her mouth completely. Replacing my dick with the condom wrapper. She rips it open with her teeth, spits the ripped part of the wrapper onto the ground, and pulls out the condom. Sliding the condom onto my dick.

She looks up at me through her thick eyelashes."Th ere you go, big guy. Ready for the ride of your life?"

Holy shit, she is confident. That is the sexiest thing I have ever heard in my life. I give her a two-finger salute.

"Ready and at your service, Ma'am."

I nudge my tip at her entrance and look at her to let her stop me. The only thing I see from her is the fire burning in her eyes and a desire as strong as mine.

I enter her slowly, giving her time to adjust to my size. She nods slightly to let me know she is ready for more, and I slowly continue to enter her until her warmth fully sheathes me. My eyes rolled to the back of my head, and a groan came out of my throat. She feels better than I could ever have imagined. This woman is a fucking sex Goddess.

"Holy fuck, Azúcar. You are so tight. I'm going to move now. Is that ok?"

I can hear her let out the breath she was holding and nod at me. I start to move in and out of her slowly. She bucks her hips up to meet me thrust for thrust. I pick up the speed and get rewarded with a sound similar to a squeak. When we start to pick up speed, Olivia reaches up to me, grabs my throat, and then flips us so that she is straddling me. She stares at me mischievously and starts to ride my cock like she has been doing this forever. Squeezing my throat to cut off my air slightly. I have never in my life had a woman cut off my air like this. I also never expected to like it. But Olivia seems to surprise me at every moment of every day.

I start to feel my balls draw up into my stomach. I pull her down so I can whisper in her ear.

"*Come with me, Azúcar.*"

Right at that moment, her pussy clenched around me so perfectly, and she came apart around me. I fill the condom right after she finishes her orgasm. Just as I told her, her juices are sliding down my shaft and covering my balls in everything that is Olivia. She falls to the side, and we lie there in the afterglow of our orgasms.

I get up, head to the bathroom, and clean myself up. I wet a rag in hot water so it is a comfortable, warm temperature when I return to Olivia. I climb back into bed and look at her sprawled out so beautifully.

"Can I clean you up, Azúcar?" I want to make sure I have all of her permissions.

"You just gave me the best orgasm of my life, and now you are asking for permission to clean me up?" She cocks an eyebrow at me. I sit there and just stare at her. I don't know how to reply because that is exactly what I am doing.

"Yes, Alex. Please clean me up, then return to bed so we can go to bed." She yawns and spreads her legs further so I can clean her up. I slowly and gently wipe up each thigh, then from her ass all the way up to clit, making sure not to miss a centimeter. She moans in satisfaction. I put the rag in the dirty clothes hamper next to Olivia's closet and get back in her bed.

Pulling her back into my chest, I bury my face into her hair and kiss her head.

"Goodnight, Azúcar," I whisper into her hair. The only reply I get is a soft snore.

Chapter Sixteen

Olivia

When I wake up the following day, I first thank whatever higher power is above that I don't have work today. I am sore in all the right places. I reached over to find the other side of the bed empty and cold; of course, he had run off. I look at my clock, and it's II am. Wow! I haven't slept that long in a long time. Alex must have worn me out last night. When I stretch, something crinkles under my arm. I see a piece of paper folded in half with my name written on it sitting on the pillow.

AZÚCAR,

I'M SORRY, BUT I HAD TO LEAVE EARLY THIS MORNING. I HAD TO BE AT WORK BY 7 A.M. YOU LOOKED TOO BEAUTIFUL SLEEPING TO WAKE UP. I KISSED YOU ON THE HEAD BEFORE I LEFT. I HAD THE MOST AMAZING NIGHT LAST NIGHT.

THANK YOU

HOPING TO SLEEP NEXT TO YOU AGAIN SOON.

ALEX

Azúcar? I remember him calling me that multiple times last night. What the fuck does it even mean. When I pull up Google, I look up the translation, Sugar. I wonder why he calls me 'sugar'. I will have to ask him the next time I see him. I wonder when the next time will be. In his note, he says 'soon,' but what is his definition of 'soon'? He will be in my bed again tonight if I have it my way. That has to be the best sleep I have had in a long time.

I finally get out of bed and go to the kitchen. I put a pod in the coffee maker and wait for it to brew the liquid life into a cup. When my coffee finally finished, I pulled up my social media and started scrolling through all the posts. Nothing is exciting - drama and pregnancies - it seems. I log off and grab my book from the side table. As soon as I am cozy and ready to dive into my book, my phone buzzes on the table. I jump and spill my coffee all over the front of me. Fucking great! Just what I need today, burnt titties with a side of irritation to start my day off right.

I grab my phone and see my twin's name on the screen: Oliver. He is still in our hometown in New York, working as the CFO for a major corporation.

> Oliver: Hey, sis! I'm attending a conference in San Diego next month. Can I stay with you?

Fuck yes! Twin time! I can't wait. It has been two years since I have seen my twin. He has been swamped becoming the new CFO, and my shifts at the station have been shitty, so this will give us time to catch up, and it's right next to our birthdays! Growing up, we were inseparable; we had always been best friends, and it weirded everyone out. Apparently, if your twin is the opposite gender, you can't be best friends with them. We said fuck that rule.

> Me: Fuck yeah, you can! I can't wait. Could you send me the dates when you get them?

As I texted my brother, I remembered my shirt was wet from coffee. Now that it's cooling off, you can absolutely see my bra through this shirt. I need to shower before I can run any errands planned for today.

I go to the bathroom, heat the water, and remove my coffee-stained clothes. When I finally look up in the mirror, I look thoroughly fucked; my hair is a rat's nest, my eyes are sparkling, and my lips still look swollen.

Last night was a great time; I am glad I went against my better judgment and went to the diner with Alex that first night. It has been a long time since I have had a smile this big on my face.

I wish at the end of the night we didn't have to stop that Andrew fucker. His arrogant ass blows my mind. How could he possibly think he did nothing wrong when he kicked Rachel in the stomach?

Sometimes, I feel like I should have gone into forensic psychology. I want to know why these people think the way they do. Why is their fucked up brain saying these things are ok? Maybe I will have to find someone to ask about it. I don't have the patience to talk to people like that. I don't have the caring nature needed to speak kindly to criminals.

I'm walking downtown, taking in all the shops around. I don't need anything for myself, but we are in October, and not only is my birthday and my twin's birthday coming up, but we have Thanksgiving and Christmas. I need to buy all my gifts while I have time off.

I walk around trying to think of something to get my twin for our birthday, and honestly, I can't think of anything. We both don't care for gifts, but we try. Maybe I'll tell him, let's get a gag gift for our birthday. That will be fun, and we'll have good laughs and create memories that will last forever.

I walk up to a sex store, and looking in the window, I can see a display in the back with dildos of all shapes and sizes; that's when an idea hits me! I am going to buy Oliver a massive dildo for his birthday! The door jingles when I walk into the little store, and all eyes are on me.

"Hi, Sweetheart. Welcome in. What can I help you find?" She is so kind; why am I so embarrassed? I am a grown woman; I shouldn't be embarrassed.

I cough nervously. "Um, yeah. I am looking for the most ridiculous dildo you have in the store. I am looking for a birthday gift for my twin brother." She doesn't even flinch. She jumps up and claps her hands. "Yay!" she squeals. "I love gag gifts!"

She walks over to the display table that I was looking at through the window. A sign says, *"Take your fantasies to the next level."* That's when I knew I had made the right choice to come here. The nerves are disappearing as I look through the dildos. There is everything from a wolf dragon dildo to a Kracken dildo, even an alien dildo. Then, the perfect dildo comes into view. It is a Krampus gold at the top and ombres to green on the penis part. There is a black base with a suction cup on it. I look at the size, and holy shit, it is 20.25 inches circumference of the base! And the head is 7.9 inches! This thing is massive! It is 11.9 inches in total length! It is absolutely perfect! Oliver is also obsessed with everything Krampus. This will make all his fantasies come true!

I grab the Krampus dick and turn to the clerk. "This one is perfect, please." Her eyes light up, and she turns beet red in the face. "Um. Great choice!" she says, and I swear I hear her say I know from experience under her breath as she walks away. She rings me up, puts it in a brown paper bag, and then wraps it in tissue paper. I might leave it like this for Oliver since it's already wrapped up. I debated on telling Oliver I was giving a gag gift, but fuck that! This is way better as a surprise.

Chapter Seventeen

Rachel

"Hey, Get up!" A yell startled me awake. I sit up and look at Andrew.

"What's going on? Why are you yelling?" I stretch and yawn as Andrew paces back and forth in front of our bed. He must be drunk or high, or both; his eyes are bloodshot, and he is bumping into everything as he walks, looking around like the boogeyman will jump out at any time.

"Get up! We need to go! Now!" I can hear the panic in his voice.

"Andrew, what is going on? Why are we rushing? Where are we going?" I am starting to panic with him. A sting radiates from my cheek. When my mind finally connected to what happened, I realized that Andrew had slapped me. This was not the first time he had hit me, though it was the first time that all I could feel was rage over the pain.

"Why the fuck do you always have to question me? I said that we are leaving, which means we are leaving. So, get your ass up and move!" He marches into the living room and continues to pace in there.

I walk to the kitchen, still processing what's happening, while getting ice for my cheek. Fuck him, I don't want to leave. I just graduated and started my job at one of the best Law firms in San Diego. Why should I have to move? I shouldn't have to put my dreams and ambitions on hold because he most likely did something dumb and got into trouble with the wrong people. He had already had his drug dealer come to our house before because he didn't pay. When that shit show happened, he tried to trade me for his debt. I didn't realize he could be so stupid, but here we are.

"NO!" I say sternly. The confidence in my voice takes Andrew and me by surprise.

Andrew tilts his head slightly, "What did you just say to me?"

I straightened my back, looked him dead in the eyes, and mustered up as much confidence as possible. "I said no, Andrew. I won't be leaving. I started my job here, and...." Another smack hit my other cheek. Tears rolled down my cheeks from the sting, but I wiped them away before he could see them because I refused to let him see me cry over him anymore.

"You don't decide what is happening here bitch! You will do as I say when I say! You have no choice in this matter. If you keep up this back-talking, we will have further issues to handle, and I don't have any fucking

time for that bullshit right now, so go to the room, pack a
bag, and get your fat ass back out here before your smart
ass mouth gets you hurt worse."

"Obviously, you didn't hear me, Andrew! I am not going with you!" I have never seen Andrew spin around so
fast in my life. He comes charging at me; I back up until
I am flush with the counter, and I grab the first thing my
hand can find to defend myself: A knife from last night
when I cut the tops off my strawberries for a snack.

Perfect.

When Andrew raises his fist to punch me, I swing my
arm and shove the knife deep into his throat, right in
his carotid artery. When he puts his hand to his throat,
he feels my hand wrapped around the knife, and his
eyes widen when he realizes what is happening. I rip the
knife from his throat, and blood sprays out everywhere.
I sit there and watch the life drain from Andrew's eyes,
the blood running down his neck and chest, and listen
to the gurgling of his lungs, trying to get air. What surprised me most was that I didn't feel bad about what
I had done. The knife in my hand feels right. Andrew
deserved a much slower death, but I won't be the one to
bring him back to life to do that to him. I will just leave
the dead where they are.

I know I need to leave this apartment and find a way
to clean up this mess. But first, I am going to take off
these clothes, burn them, and then shower. No one needs
to know about this. I'll take the knife, so the evidence
isn't there, but I need to go far away from here. But
where will I go?

After I shower, I pack an overnight bag with one suit outfit for work, some leggings, underwear, a spare bra, and my lucky red heels. I rush into the bathroom, grab my hairbrush and toothbrush, and zip up the bag. I am out the door within minutes and walking towards the beach about five miles away. Finally, I sit down on a bench to catch my breath and process everything that has happened.

FUCK! I stabbed someone! I murdered someone! How the fuck am I supposed to be a Lawyer and hold up the law when I broke the law. What the fuck!

I pulled out my phone and searched my contacts for anyone willing to help me. Thanks to Andrew cutting off all my friends, I no longer have anywhere to go. Then I freeze. The name Alex García is on my phone. There is no way that this is the same Alex who helped me at the hospital, is it? I hover my finger over the little green button, contemplating whether I should call him or not. Before I can talk myself out of it, I close my eyes, jam my finger onto the little green button, and put the phone to my ear.

After the second ring, he answers.

"Hello"

"Um. Hey. Alex? It's Rachel. The girl you helped get to the hospital." Well, that was brilliant... not... I could have said anything else.

"I knew it was you, Rachel. I put my number in your phone before you left the hospital in case you needed me again. So what made you call me?" He is so calm and collected. What will he think when I tell him the truth?

Can I tell him the truth? Will he turn me in if he finds out that I killed Andrew? Will he think I am crazy when he discovers my real feelings about how I liked it? While I am lost in my spiral of questions.

I am snapped back into the conversation when Alex asks, "Rachel, are you OK? What made you call? Are you hurt again? Did Andrew do something? Where are you at? I will come to get you."

"So I am at South Mission Beach. I am not with Andrew. I was wondering if you could pick me up and possibly take me to a motel. Andrew and I are no longer together and don't have a place to stay."

I heard rustling on the other end of the phone. There was something about getting keys and a jingle. I assume Alex is getting in the car.

"Hey, stay where you are. I will grab you, take you back to my house, and figure out a plan."

The tires squeal in the background when Alex says, "I'm on my way!"

Chapter Eighteen

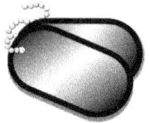

Alex

I grab my keys, run out of the house, get into my new 4Runner, and start it up, peeling out of the driveway with a squeal. My heart is racing; I don't know what to expect, and of course, she is at the beach, fifteen minutes from the base, when there is no traffic. This is when I wish I could have a hovercar. Just zoom past every fucker on the ground.

When I finally got onto the bridge heading towards I-5, I asked, "Rachel, are you still with me?" I could hear her breathing on the other side of the phone, but I needed to hear her voice.

"Yeah, I am here. I am just staring at the waves. I could get lost in the sound of waves." I breathe. She sounds fine. The only thing I can tell from her voice is that she is tired. I will take her home, make her some food, and then let her rest. We can plan what to do after that. We can figure out what happened between her and

Andrew. And I will figure out where he is and end his ass.

I pulled up to the beach twenty minutes later; there was some traffic, but it was not bad. Instantly, I see Rachel sitting on a log in the sand, staring into the water, phone still up to her ear. I unbuckled my seatbelt and hung up the phone. She didn't even realize I hung up until I walked behind her. She has a big overnight bag with her. She wears black leggings, a grey sweatshirt hanging off her shoulder, glasses, and no makeup. Her hair is down and wet as if she just got out of the shower. Physically, she looks fine, and that alone makes the pulling in my chest lighten a bit.

"Hey," I say as I walk up towards her. She looked at me with a sheepish smile, and her blue eyes seemed almost grey with no sign of life in them. That's when I saw the handprints on her cheeks. I reached out my hand to grab her chin, and she flinched. I pulled back immediately.

"Hey," she said back. She stands up, grabs her bag, and slings it over her shoulder. She walks up to me slowly, with caution.

"What happened? Why do you have handprints on your cheeks? Did Andrew do this?" She locks away and won't answer the questions.

"Don't worry. It's all taken care of. I'm ok. Promise."
She says as she holds out her pinky for a pinky promise.
I grab her pinky, and she kisses her thumb. I look at her
with a questioning look.

"It's to seal the pinky promise, " she says as if it were
no big deal, and everyone should know that. I kiss my
thumb, too, and she pushes our thumbs together and
smiles at me.

She sounds so sure about everything, but I swear
something must have happened. I can feel it. I swear to
fucking God! I will skin Andrew alive! I will torture him
so badly that he will be wishing for the sweet release of
death!

I motion for her to go ahead of me. She nods at me
and starts to walk towards the car. My mind is going a
thousand miles an hour, and I think the one thing I told
myself I would never think!

I NEED TO ASK MY GRANDFATHER FOR HELP.....

We pull up to my house after a fifteen-minute car ride
of silence. All Rachel did was look out the window, lost
in thought. I kill the engine and unbuckle, looking over
at Rachel, who hasn't moved a muscle, and it's starting
to worry me. I walk around to her side of the car and
open her door for her, but she doesn't move. I offer my
hand to her, and she continues staring into space, not
even noticing that I am next to her. I bend to unbuckle
her seat belt, and that is when she finally looks at me,
blinking out of thought. Her eyes show nothing, but I
have a strong gut feeling that it wasn't nothing.

"Hey, Mi Muñeca, I'm going to pick you up and carry you into the house. Is that okay?" She gives me a very faint nod of approval. I bend down and scoop her into my arms, grabbing her bag with my free hand, slinging it over my shoulder, and using my hip to shut the door.

I walk into my house and through the living room to get to the guest bedroom, where I lay Rachel on the queen-sized bed when we enter. "Do you want to tell me what happened or rest first?" She looks at me and shakes her head.

"That's okay. We will get through this together. I am not going anywhere, but I need to know what happened to be able to help you." She grabs my hand and closes her eyes. Her breathing turns into soft snores almost instantly, so I slowly remove my hand from hers and grab the blanket from the foot of the bed. I lay it over her and quietly leave the room. She needs some rest.

As I close the door, I turn and head to my office. I need to make this call even though I don't want to. I can't get my hands dirty without jeopardizing my career, and regardless of how long it has been since I talked to my grandfather, he will always help me when I ask.

I go to my bar cart and pour a hefty amount of whiskey before taking a sip and savoring the burn. I pull out my phone and scroll through my contacts. My finger hovers over the call button. I take a deep breath and click it. A deep, husky voice answers on the other end at the second ring.

"Lopez García!"

"Hey, it's me. I need help with something."

"Mi Nieto, what can I help you with?" My grandfather says in a surprisingly chipper tone.

"There is a guy named Andrew Starr; he was in jail for domestic violence a couple of months ago for kicking his pregnant girlfriend into a brick building and killing the baby. I need anything and everything you can get on this man." My grandfather doesn't reply for a while, and it starts to make me nervous.

"Alright, Mi Nieto, I got everything about him pulled up. What would you like to do? Do you just want his file? Do you want me to send some people to get him hung up in a warehouse? Do you want me to make him disappear? What exactly is the outcome you are looking for?" He replied that it was no big deal and that he hadn't just asked me how I wanted to handle Andrew.

"The warehouse works great for me. Thanks." You know, I never wanted to be in the family business. I never wanted to take my grandfather's place, but since he didn't have a boy and my mom had me, I am the next Heir. I don't want it. I never have, but being the heir to the Cartel does have its benefits. Like being able to get what you want done, no matter what it is.

"So, are you going to tell me about her?"

"No, I am good. Thank you for your help. Send me a text when it's ready for me." I hung up the phone before he could ask any more questions. I put my phone back in my pocket and returned to the guest bedroom.

I sit in the chair in the corner of the room and watch Rachel sleep. Making sure her chest continues to rise and fall, just like I did in the hospital with her. Making

sure that she sleeps soundly and knows she is safe in
my house.

Chapter Nineteen

Rachel

I woke up and looked around the room. I have no clue where I am or how I got here. I get up and wander over to the in-suite bathroom to use the restroom and brush my teeth. How did I end up here? I should figure out where I am first, and then everything else afterward.

The last I remember was.... OH SHIT! I killed Andrew. I stabbed him. I look over at the toilet and rush to get over it before the contents of my stomach empty. I am a murderer.

NO!!! I was defending myself! He has abused me so much for the past five years, using me as his personal punching bag! He got what was coming to him! Fuck him! I am glad I am finally done with his ass.

But where am I?

How did I end up here?

Whose house is this?

I walk into the hallway and turn right because I see more light coming from that direction. As I walk further, the smell of bacon invades my senses, and my stomach grumbles. When was the last time I ate? How long did I sleep? My neck and body are stiff, and it feels like I have been asleep for days.

When I turn the corner, I see a shirtless Alex cooking in the kitchen! His muscles are absolutely amazing, so defined and beautiful. The tattoos all over his arms are on full display for my personal viewing, and I will gladly stand here and stare. His hair is wet as if he just got out of the shower, and honestly, my mouth waters at the sight. This man is sex on legs. I walk to the kitchen and see that he is wearing only grey sweatpants, and everything down south is perfectly outlined, from the delicious V cut to the outline of his very large bulge in his crotch. If this is how big he is when he is soft... I am extremely nervous to see how big he is when he is hard. Lord, save my life if that ever comes near my entrance.

"Good morning, Cariña. How are you feeling this morning?"

I have no clue what he just called me, but hearing him speak Spanish was sexy as hell, and I had to rub my thighs together to control the need building in my core. "I am OK, but I was not quite sure what happened. I woke up freaking out about where I was, but once I saw you, all those worries went away."

"Well, I am glad I can comfort you and make you feel safe! Are you hungry?" Of course, when he asked if I was hungry, my stomach growled so loudly that the neighbors could probably hear it.

A deep rumble of laughter comes from deep within Alex's chest. "I'll take that as a yes. Sit down; food should be done in a few minutes." He turns back around and goes back to cooking on the stove.

I sit at the small, dark, wooden dining room table. It has four chairs around it. I take the one closest to the wall to watch Alex while he works. I admire all that he has on display that I probably shouldn't be looking at after what happened with Andrew, but who the fuck cares. Andrew is dead, and Alex is standing here half-naked. I don't know if it makes me a bad person, but I don't feel bad about what happened with Andrew. I honestly feel like Andrew's death is all a dream, and he is going to come get me and take me back home, and I will be punished for dreaming of stabbing him. If someone finds out that I stabbed him, I know for a fact that I won't make it out alive.

I hear something fall outside. I fall out of my chair and curl into myself in the corner. Every little sound has me jumping since I have been back from the hospital, but right now, it is even worse. I get snapped out of my dark spiral by a plate being placed in front of me. "Eat up, Cariña. You look like you haven't had anything to eat since the last time I saw you."

"Ummm. Thanks." I look up at him and give him a scared smile.

We finish breakfast, and I grab my plate to take it to the sink to wash it. As I came back to grab Alex's plate, he grabbed my wrist to stop me.

"You don't need to grab my dishes. I can take care of it. Just set yours in the sink, and I will wash them once I get up." He smiles at me with that pantie-melting smile of his, and all I want to do is bend down and kiss him. I keep telling myself it's too soon after Andrew, but I have been checked out of that relationship for at least a year. The least I could do was move on. I don't know what has gotten into me. One minute, I fall out of my chair because I hear something fall; the next, I am drooling over Alex, ready to pounce on him.

I walk over to the sink, rinse off my plate, and put it in the dishwasher. When I turn around, Alex is rolling his eyes at me.

"You know you are a brat, right?" He raises his eyebrow at me.

"Yeah, it's not the first time I have been called that." I walk over towards him at the table and lean down, where my lips are only an inch away from his. "And what are you going to do about it, tough guy?" I taunt him.

Alex stands up fast, and I turn and run up the stairs. I haven't been up this way since my guest bedroom is downstairs, but I guess I will find my way around quickly. I climb the stairs, turn left, and run further down the hall. I can hear Alex's feet pounding on the ground behind me. I have to make a decision quickly.

I open the door to the right and quietly close it behind me. Holy shit, I must be in the master bedroom. It's HUGE! In the center is a four-post dark oak bed that looks bigger than a king bed. A bay window is located to the left, with a recliner chair in front of it. To the right of the bed is a dark oak dresser. To the left of the dresser are two doors. I hurry, open the first door, and walk into the bathroom. Once again, I try to close the door quietly. As soon as I hear it click, I turn, get into the shower, and squat in the corner.

I hear the door across the hall slam open. Then, the master bedroom door slams open. I am not sure why I started this game with all the times Andrew chased me through the house to beat the shit out of me, but I am not scared, probably because Andrew is dead, and this is Alex, but my anxiety that I usually have is nowhere to be found.

Alex makes his way into the bathroom, and I hold in a giggle, trying to escape my lips. As Alex passed the shower, I stepped out as quietly as possible and jumped on his back.

"Gotcha!" I say, kissing his cheek and then climbing off of him.

He turns and grabs me by my hips. "So you want to run from me, Cariña? You think this is funny?" He pulls me towards him, where his very stiff cock is pushing against my stomach.

I bat my eyes at him innocently. "I mean…" I say, shrugging, and try to turn around and walk away.

"Oh no, you don't, brat!" He grabs me by my waist, turns me around, and flings me over his shoulder. All I do is giggle as he walks towards the bed. The next thing I knew, I was flying through the air and landing with a oomph on the bed.

When I looked up, I saw that Alex was completely serious. "Are you ok with this? I won't do anything that you're not okay with, Rachel. So you need to tell me now to stop. I know you just left your relationship with Andrew, and I don't want to push you too far." The worry in his voice is prominent, and I want to reassure him that I am completely on board with this. Yes, I know I may sound like a whore, but I am a free woman now. I can do what I want or, in this case, who I want.

I sit up, wrap my hands around his neck, and pull him towards me as I lean back on the bed, fusing our lips together. Alex moaned in my mouth, and I pulled him closer, feeling his erection stiffen on me as I grind up to get some friction on my throbbing pussy. I have never felt a need like this in my life. Alex grabs my wrists and pulls them over my head.

"I need your words, Muñeca. I need to have your complete consent before we do anything."

"Please, Alex," I begged shamelessly. "I need you. Right now!" I am a squirming, panting mess right now, and I couldn't care less how impatient I am being. He did this to me, so he has to deal with it.

I guess my words were the magic key because the next thing I knew, Alex shifted onto his knees and reached out his hand for me to grab. "Sit up. You have too many clothes on," he says, reaching for the hem of my shirt and pulling it over my head in one swift motion. I began to pull down my pajama pants and underwear. Hey, look! My clothes are still in one piece. That's a new experience. No! NO Rachel! No bringing up even the thought of that shitty past.

As my eyes met Alex's, all the nerves from earlier and memories of my past disappeared and turned into butterflies of anticipation fluttering in my stomach. My need for him overpowered every emotion I could possibly feel.

Giving me a quick kiss, he gets off the bed, walks over to the bedside table, and pulls out a condom. He places it between his teeth and holds it while he makes quick work of his sweatpants, then climbs up onto the bed, fitting himself perfectly right between my thighs.

He takes the condom out of his mouth and puts it on the bed next to me. Shifting back to take in the view of me, his eyes sparkle with want and hunger. Something that never shone in Andrew's eyes. All he ever cared about was himself and how he was going to get off; there was never hunger in his eyes, never an actual want for me. He just wanted a place to put his cock; that's why he was mad about the baby. It would have taken my attention, and he wouldn't have been able to use me whenever he wanted.

"Hey," Alex whispered to me. Tilting my head up with his finger. "I see that beautiful brain of yours working in overdrive right now. No thinking, just feeling." He bends down and captures my lips again, and thoughts of Andrew disappear.

Alex's hands explored every inch of my body, starting at my face and making their way down my neck to my chest as he groped each breast with the perfect amount of pressure. Making his way down to my stomach until he was going over my hips and to the outside of my thighs.

He looks up from his exploration with a question in his eyes. I know he is asking me if it's ok to continue. I look back at him, confused because this is all new territory for me.

"Muñeca, I will not do anything that you don't want me to do. I will always ask for your permission. Consent is critical to me; you will never be forced to do anything you don't want to again." He looks at me with the most genuine look in his eyes. It makes me melt even more under his touch.

"I trust you, Alex. I want to do this." I reply, then grab his face to make him look me in the eyes. "You are not Andrew. I will never think you are. You are completely different and have been nothing but amazing to me. I like you, Alex. Please make me feel good. Please make my mind stop going a thousand miles an hour. I need you."

That was enough information to convince Alex to continue. To let him know I was serious. He bent down and kissed me with so much passion that it made my head spin. He continued his hands down the outside of my thighs, then moved to the inside and up until he was cupping my very wet pussy in his hands.

"You are so ready for me, aren't you?" He mumbles into my mouth, then kisses me harder. The only reply I could give was a moan as he started to rub slow torturous circles on my clit. I put my fingers in his hair while he works magic on me.

Slipping one finger into my slick heat and curling his finger to hit the exact spot that makes me see stars, my body arches in pleasure.

"Alex! Oh my god! Yes, please! Right there!" Pleasure radiates throughout my body, causing my mind to stop thinking and just feel.

I am starting to climb the mountain of bliss when Alex pulls out his finger. I look at him with my mouth hanging open.

"Why would you stop? I was so close!" I complain to him, and he laughs at me.

"Because Muñeca, The first time I make you come apart, will be on my cock. You cum with me!" He has heat and hunger in his eyes.

"Well, that's hot!" My excitement bubbled to the surface. "If I am going to cum on your cock, then I am going to need you to get inside of me so I can feel every inch of you." My dirty words flowed perfectly out of my mouth to make him groan.

"Yes, Ma'am." This is the only reply I got before he grabbed the condom from beside me and ripped it open. Before he can put it on, I grab it from his hands.

"Allow me," I wink at him and slowly roll the condom over his length, giving it a gentle squeeze when I finish, and watch his eyes roll to the back of his head. Placing my hands on his shoulders, I push him back so he is lying down on the bed. I straddle him and slowly lower myself on him, inch by torturous inch.

I forgot how good sex could feel when you actually want to do it! This man feels so perfect in me. Once I am fully seated on him, I look at him with heat in my eyes. I slowly rise and drop down with a little more force, causing his length to hit my G-spot. As we pick up speed, he grabs me by the shoulder and flips me over, taking complete control of the situation, and I am here for it. Grabbing my legs, he puts my ankles up on his shoulders and pounds into me with a brutal rhythm.

"ALLLLEEEEXXXXX!" I scream as I feel my orgasm coming on strong.

"Hold on, Muñeca, I am almost there!" He says as he starts to pound even faster.

One thrust.

After two thrusts, I feel his body start to tighten up.

"Come with me, Muñeca, now!" He growls with one final thrust, and I fall over the edge of bliss. He finishes and leans down to place his sweaty forehead against mine while we try to catch our breath.

"Holy shit! That was amazing. Thank you, Alex. I needed that." I say, reaching up to grab the back of his neck and look into his eyes.

"The pleasure was all mine, Muñeca." Kissing my forehead one last time, he rolls off of me and heads to the bathroom to dispose of the used condom. I hear the toilet flush and the water run before he comes out with a wet rag.

"Can I clean you up, Muñeca?" He asks sincerely.

I nod in response and then have to ask the question that has been on my mind all day. "What is Muñeca? I have heard you call me that many times today. What does it mean?"

He chuckles at me and says, " It means doll because your face reminds me of a doll. They are so perfect, smooth, and beautiful." I can feel the heat go straight to my cheeks.

"Thank you again for taking care of me, Alex. In every way you have." I kiss him before I lean down and snuggle into his chest. He whispers something back, but sleep is so close that I can't hear him.

Chapter Twenty

Olivia

It has been a week since Alex came back to my apartment with me. I can't get any moment of that night out of my head. It was pure bliss. Alex has been busy with work, but we have texted back and forth a couple of times. It was a short conversation, but I didn't mind. I am not a very big texting person anyway; I prefer a face-to-face conversation to read emotions and the room. I guess that's just what my dad ingrained in my and Oliver's heads since we were little.

Don't trust anyone.
Don't turn your back.
Always have each other.
Keep your guard up at all times.

I put on my undershirt and slicked my hair back into a bun. I also put on some eyeliner and mascara to make my face look less like death. At this point, the whole process of putting on my uniform is muscle memory. My mind doesn't have to think, which is one of the many reasons I love wearing a uniform to work.

My mind keeps going back to Oliver coming to San Diego. I'm curious about his meeting and why he has to come here from New York. Don't get me wrong, I am grateful that Oliver is coming to visit, but I am nosy why. My brother and I are yin and yang. I need him to help my brain function. Some say our relationship is too co-dependent, but what do you expect when you share everything with someone for your whole life? We never gave a shit about what people said, about how close we are. He is my better and smarter half. I am just the fighter.

After one last look at myself in the mirror, I head down the stairs to the garage while searching for my keys. I trip over the last step and catch myself on the brick wall at the bottom of the stairs. Grace was not my strong suit. I am fantastic at tripping over air.

I get my balance, grab my keys, and go to the back of the parking lot. I don't park up front because some families or elders need those spots more than I do. I can walk further to my car to help a mom with three screaming kids as she tries to get them up the stairs.

I see around ten dead crows on the hood as I approach my car. On my windshield, there is the blood that looks like it was finger-painted, that said.

FUCKING PIG! KEEP YOUR NOSE OUT OF OUR SHIT!

I looked around the garage to see if anyone was there. This message looks like a teenager wrote it, but there is no telling nowadays. I stuck my finger in the blood, and it's still warm, meaning this finger painting was recent. Whoever did this knows I am a cop and that I am investigating something. I have been on many cases, so it could be anyone. But who would come to my home to leave me a message? Someone deranged, for sure.

I took pictures of my car, removed the crows from my hood, and took them to the nearest trash can in the parking garage. I took three trips to the trash can to remove all twelve birds from my car. I was close to my guess of ten. Is the number twelve a sign of something?

I will take my car to the car wash before I head to the office. The last thing I need is for people to start asking me questions and to take me off the Los Comos case. This is a case I have worked my ass off to get onto, and they finally trust me enough to put me on it. I refuse to let them down.

Once I enter the office, I sit at my desk, flopping into my chair and looking at the massive stack of files on my desk. Who the fuck piled my desk. Ugh. With an eye roll, I grab the first file off the top of the stack, and my heart drops. There is a picture of a little girl in the file who can't be older than ten. She has big blue eyes, blonde hair that looks like it hasn't been brushed or washed ever that flows down to her butt. She is in a dress covered in dirt, and she seems like she hasn't had a bite of food in months. This has to be a picture of her now that she is captured. Flipping the page, I see more information on her: the missing person's report, school reports, medical reports, birth certificate, and a family photo. She looks to be the middle child of five kids and the only girl. The picture shows her in the most adorable baby-blue dress; her hair is braided in French braids, and she has the biggest smile in the world. Her four brothers are wearing matching jeans and white shirts, staring at her and smiling. This picture is so pure. I bet her family is worried sick. I know if it were my kid or sibling, I would be. I couldn't even imagine what would happen if Oliver went missing.

I took a second to gather myself before grabbing the next file, and it was a little boy. I looked at his birth certificate and realized he had just had a birthday; he was barely three. My blood goes cold. He is Hispanic and honestly reminds me of Alex with his dark hair and big brown eyes. In the picture, he has the biggest smile and a dimple on his right cheek; he is the cutest little kid I have ever seen. You wouldn't know that he was in captivity if it weren't for the lack of meat on his bones and the dirty clothes, just like in the previous picture. I keep flipping through and see a picture of him and a woman I assume is his mom. It was just the two of them. Holy shit. I couldn't imagine losing my son. I would burn the whole world to the ground to find my kid.

I continued flipping through all the other files for another two hours. There are a total of one hundred and three files. Of the one hundred and three files, I have thirty males, forty women, and thirty-three children.

All of these files are of different ages, races, and genders. Apparently, Los Comos likes everyone; it doesn't matter what kind of person they are willing to sell anyone. All of these files have a current picture of them and one of them before they were taken. I am not sure how they got the current photos of them, but they all look like they haven't had any food for a month, need a shower, and are in disgustingly dirty clothes.

This case is going to be harder to handle than I expected. I knew they were trafficking, but I thought it would be more women than children; apparently, I was way off. There are almost the same number of women, men, and children in these files. There is no way Lopez-García is doing this alone, which means I need to take down all of them, even if it's the last thing I do.

I have never felt so determined! I refuse to let these people down. I need to get them back to their families, and I will do anything in my power to make that happen.

Chapter Twenty-One

Alex

This Monday has been the longest Monday in what seems like forever. I am sitting at my desk, staring at my computer, with nothing to do, but they won't let us leave. It was stupid, and to add on top of that, my mind also won't shut the fuck up; It keeps going back to Olivia and Rachel. How did I end up where I am with both of these women? Olivia and I went on a date and then had amazing sex. The chemistry was electrifying; now we talk on a regular basis, and I am planning another date with her soon.

Rachel is still living at my house. She is starting to open up to me after only three days of being here. I wasn't expecting her to open up so fast, even if we also had mind–blowing sex. She told me how Andrew used to expect her to go to school and have the house in pristine condition. He would smack or punch her if she didn't have good grades or the house was not tidy. She told me she always had to wear makeup to cover the bruises when going to class or an internship.

She told me at the hospital that she was about to graduate from college with her law degree and was planning to get set up with a firm here in San Diego. I am not sure if she got a job or not; I should probably ask because if she does have a job, she needs to take a leave of absence for all the bullshit Andrew just put her through. What I am sitting here currently pondering in my head is why she hasn't mentioned what made her call me. What did Andrew do to cause her to be so scared to talk? Every time I bring it up, she shuts down, her blue eyes go almost grey, and her skin goes pale like she will get sick. After the second time that happened, I stopped asking. There is nothing that important that I have to keep pushing her.

My phone vibrated on the table. It was a text from an unknown number with the two words I had been waiting for. I knew they were the start of something I wanted nothing to do with, but I had to do it.

UNKNOWN: CALL ME!

I headed up to Sir's office to ask to leave. This is not a conversation I can have at work.

I knocked on the door.

"Yeah?" His voice booms from behind the door.

I open the door and stick my head in.

"Hey, Sir, I just got a call from my mom. She needs me to pick her up and take her to a doctor's. Is it okay for me to dip out for the day? I have done everything assigned to me, and if anything else pops up today, I can do it first thing in the morning." I word vomit. I hate lying to Sir. The man, I swear, is pure gold.

"Yeah, that is fine. I'll see you tomorrow." He says with a nod.

As soon as I was out of the building, I grabbed my helmet and put it on my head as fast as possible. I drove the speed limit on base because the last thing I needed was to be pulled over by those rent-a-cops. After going through the gate, I sped towards the nearest warehouse, my family owned. My grandfather had a transmitter to ensure no one could hear my conversations in every location we owned.

I pulled up to a bunch of abandoned warehouses and found the one in the far left corner that was ours. I rolled my bike into the warehouse with me and pulled up the number I had called more in the past week than in the last five years.

My grandfather.

On the second ring, the phone is answered.

"Lopez García!"

"Hey, it's me."

"Alejandro! So I have looked into the little problem you mentioned."

"Abuelo, I am at the warehouse. We can talk."

"Perfect, Mi Nieto. I had some friends find this Andrew guy you asked about, and what they found was quite interesting."

"Abuelo, can you please just tell me what's going on? I don't have enough energy for riddles today. Can you just get straight to the point? "

"This Andrew you were talking about was found dead in his apartment. Stab wound to the carotid artery. It's not a clean cut across the throat. It's a stab directly to the artery."

"A stab wound? Who stabbed him? You were supposed to just get the fucker for me! What do you mean, someone did the job already? I wanted to kill the fucker for hurting Rachel!!"

"My men didn't kill him. They had strict instructions not to kill him. It seems as if he has been dead for a couple of days. I am not sure who killed him, but we did take a clean-up crew to the house."

"Thank you for the clean-up crew. I will do some research to see who could have stabbed him."

"I already looked into it for you. I knew you would be curious. No one has gone in or out of the apartment besides Andrew and Rachel, and no one has been there since Rachel left on Friday."

Hmm, that's odd. That would mean that Rachel killed him or Andrew killed himself, which I highly doubt.

"Alejandro, it seems like you have a murderer in your house right now that you are warming your bed with."

I laughed a full belly laugh.

"Abuelo, first off, who warms my bed is not your concern. Second, you act like I haven't been raised around
murderers my whole life. It's like you forget that Mom
and I lived with you most of my childhood."

"Just be careful, is all I ask. And you are alive because
you lived with me. Your deadbeat father wasn't going to
protect you or your mother."

"I always am. Bye." I hung up, and now my mind is
going even faster! Every time he goes on a tangent about
my biological father, it always makes my stomach turn.
I don't know who my biological father is, and truthfully
I don't give a shit. My mom raised me just fine on her
own, and I owe that woman my whole life.

The one thing I did know was that I had to get to
my house and see Rachel. I put on my helmet, walk my
bike out of the warehouse, and head home. I need to go
into this conversation with a level head if I want to get
answers.

Chapter Twenty-Two

Olivia

"O'Connor! My office now!" The Captain yells at me. I get up from my seat, lock my computer, and head towards his office. We have some nosey fuckers in the office, and I don't need them snooping through all that I have found out about Los Comos. I know I have a great team behind me, but I don't need someone trying to take credit for my work.

I knocked on the door seal and popped my head into the office.

"Come in, O'Connor." He says in a gruff voice

"What can I do for you, Captain?"

"Please have a seat ." I sit in the chair, crossing my right knee over my left. I tap my foot as my nerves are getting the best of me. I am reviewing everything I could have done to land me in this office. I don't think I have done anything wrong. I have all the up-to-date information on Los Comos. I wonder if there's a new file I need to look into. Maybe a more solid place to start looking for these fuckers?

I am pulled out of my thoughts when the Captain clears his throat. "So, O'Connor, you have been doing great with the Los Comos case. I have been talking with people, and they have been impressed with your work. We would like to offer you a permanent position in the Investigation Unit, if that is something you are interested in. You are a great fit, and the team already loves you."

I swear I hear Captain chuckle as my jaw drops. What the fuck did he just say? This is a joke, right? This was the last thing I expected, but something I have been working my ass off to get to! It's as if all my hard work is finally being recognized. I am proving to myself and my family that I made the right decision to go into Law Enforcement, and not the Financial field.

"I would love to be a part of the Investigation Unit. That has been a dream of mine for as long as I can remember. Thank you, Captain." I stutter and make a fool of myself because I sound like a small child who got what they wanted.

"You will be moving to the FBI building downtown, where the team is. That is where you will report from now on. I will let their Captain know you agreed; we will get your paperwork ready for transfer, and you will most likely be reporting there starting Monday." My mind is going a thousand miles an hour, and I have the biggest smile on my face.

"Thank you so much, Captain. You won't regret this decision." He dismisses me from his office with a nod, and I practically skip to my desk.

I am so excited that I had to send a text to Alex.

> Me: Hey, I just got the best news!

Alex: What's up? I love great news! Also! Long time no talk, by the way.

> Me: I am officially part of the Investigation unit!!! This is my dream come true! Also, I know. I am sorry. Work has been crazy. Dinner tonight? My treat!

Alex: Congratulations! That's amazing! I am so proud of you! Dinner tonight sounds great! But how about you come to my place for dinner? It's my treat, and we get to celebrate your amazing accomplishment.

I am smiling, and so many people are starting to look my way.

Alex: Rachel is at my house right now, so I will have to explain that situation in person. Would 6 be a good time?

> Me: Sounds great! See you then! I have to start packing up my desk!

That's not what I was expecting him to say. I wonder what's happening with Rachel and why she's at Alex's house. I will have to ask him before we go inside.

When I get home from work, I shower to clean off the day; then I find my Black spaghetti-strap dress that stops mid-thigh. I put on some makeup and curled my red hair so it's not poofy like a poodle, but in ringlet curls. Looking in the mirror, I approve of my look, grab my black heels, and head for the door. I sit on the bench beside my door, strap my heels, grab my clutch and keys, and head to the garage. I am so excited for tonight. I have needed to see Alex. I have missed him. It also happens that the last time I saw him was when he blew my mind with fantastic sex. Maybe we could have a repeat of that night. I'm not sure how that would work with Rachel at the house, but if I had my way, I would have her join.

Most people don't know this, but I have had sex with more women than I have men. The only person who knows everything is Oliver, but he is my twin, so of course, he knows everything. I have never actually had a girlfriend, though; usually, it's dinner, then sex, and then we never speak again. I know I sound like a whore...

When I pull into Alex's house, he steps out onto the front porch. Looking absolutely delicious in a black long-sleeve Henley, dark denim jeans, and bare feet, his dark brown hair was styled to spike up slightly at the front. His hands were in his pockets, and he smiled from ear to ear. Damn, he is good-looking! I don't know how he takes my breath away whenever I see him. Is this a normal reaction, or should I see the doctor?

I get out of the car, pull down my dress since it started to ride up while I was driving, and walk up to his house. He wraps me in a hug and kisses the top of my head.

"Hey, beautiful." He kisses my head and then lifts my chin to kiss my lips.

Okay, I am swooning. This man has some magical spell on me, and I don't know if I even care.

Chapter Twenty-Three

Alex

I hear a car pull into the driveway and look out the front window. I see Olivia pulling up in her black Cadillac, deep in thought. I wonder what she is thinking about... I will have to get that look off her face soon. She shouldn't be thinking so hard; she should be celebrating.

I go outside to greet her and let her know what is going on with Rachel before we head in. I have the fajitas almost done, and everything else is ready to go. I let Rachel know that Olivia was coming over, and she seemed excited; she even asked me what she should wear. I rarely see a smile on Rae's face since she got here, but I admire it for as long as possible when it does make an appearance. So, I helped her pick out a dress for tonight. I am not sure if Rachel is into girls, but by the way, she was excited about Olivia coming over. I think she at least has a little girl crush she is trying to hide.

Olivia steps out of her car in the sexiest little black dress and black heels, which perfectly accentuate her legs. Her beautiful red hair is curled down her back. She looks absolutely stunning; I am surprised I don't have drool running down my chin. She walks up with the biggest smile on her face, and I wrap her in a hug.

"Hey, Beautiful!" I look down and kiss the top of her head, then lift her chin to kiss her lips. I forgot how addicting her lips felt on mine. I could get carried away with the feel of her lips on mine.

She pulls away with a smile, "Hey, yourself, handsome!"

The smile fades, and the worry takes its place. "So what happened with Rachel? Why is she staying with you? Isn't Andrew out of jail? He might come for her, and that puts you at risk." I look down at her and grab her chin, lifting her eyes to mine.

"Breath, Azúcar! She came here to get away from Andrew. Some people I know think Andrew won't be a problem anymore. She called me when she left Andrew because she had nowhere else to go. She wanted me to drop her off at a motel, but I refused to let her stay in some shitty motel when I had a house she could stay at. She is fine. We will all be fine." Her eyes shone with hope from the information I gave her. She nods, grabbing my neck to bring my face down to her. She kisses me deeply and passionately. Grabbing my shirt, she deepens the kiss and brushes her tongue against the seam of my mouth. I gladly open up, and her tongue fights mine for dominance. I love it when she is dominant; it is sexy as fuck. I would submit to her any day of the week, but that day is not today. I grab her throat and slowly squeeze until she whimpers in my mouth.

"You are only allowed to dominate when I let you dominate, Azúcar." A beautiful blush spreads along her cheeks when she nods at me and rolls her eyes.

"We will see how that works out for you. I tend to do what I want."

Someone clearing their throat behind us causes us to break apart. We both look up at the same time and see Rachel in the doorway, a blush spread across her cheeks. Someone enjoyed the show.

"Hey, Rachel, how are you doing?" Olivia said while walking up to her and embracing her in a tight hug. At first, Rachel's face looks a little uncomfortable, but then her body relaxes, and she melts into Olivia's arms with a big sigh. The contentment is unmistakable on her face. There has to be something about Olivia because the way Rachel looks right now is exactly how I feel when Olivia wraps me in a hug. This girl has something magical in her hugs.

"I am alright. Thanks for asking," she replies, looking up at Olivia with one of the most beautiful smiles. Then, grabs Olivia's hand, turns around, and leads Olivia into the house as if she owns the place. Watching those two walk hand in hand into my home makes my mind conjure up a million dirty thoughts. I have to get my head out of that space before I have a raging hard-on all through dinner.

"Hey, big guy, what's for dinner? I see it's a triple date." Olivia says over her shoulder with a wink.

A chuckle escaped my lips before I could stop it, and I shook my head. Olivia sure knew how to blurt out what she was feeling with no care.

"Fajitas, Azúcar"

Olivia looks up at me, confused. "Why do you call me that?"

"It is another term for sweet or sugar; you are sweet in many ways, so I saw it fitting."

She looked at me with a deeper questioning look, but then she shook it off and continued into the house. I have a feeling she will ask me more questions later tonight.

Olivia and Rachel sit on the bar stools at the counter, watching me cook. Like they are waiting for me to fuck up and burn the whole house down. It honestly makes me nervous.

I look up as I cut the onions. "What?"

They both look at each other and smile.

"Nothing", they say in unison.

"Mhmmm, sure, I believe that one... I feel like you two are planning something that is not very promising for me," I say over my shoulder.

"We would never; I don't even know how you could think we were capable of something that evil." Rachel giggles.

I turn around, roll my eyes at the girls, and then start cutting up the bell peppers. These girls are something else, and it might be my death, but I am here for it. Death by two extremely hot women sounds like a pretty good death to me.

Chapter Twenty-Four

Rachel

The Fajita tasted amazing, the conversations flowed smoothly, and the effervescent energy radiated through the house. Having Olivia over seemed completely natural and calming. I am glad I finally got to talk to Olivia alone and thank her for what she did when Andrew kicked me.

I see why Alex likes her. She is so easy to talk to, and she is absolutely stunning with her Auburn hair that flows down her back, eyes that I can't quite tell if they are blue or green, and her creamy pale skin with a slight dusting of freckles on her face. She also has a beautiful landscape sleeve tattoo. She looks like an absolute goddess.

I have never been interested in women, but there is something about Olivia. I have always admired beautiful women, but the feeling of Olivia's hand in mine felt so right. As soon as she hugged me, a spark of life entered me. It was like pieces of me were falling into place. It was bizarre; I didn't know how to feel about it, so I embraced it.

When we finished dinner, Olivia took our plates to the sink. "You don't have to do the dishes. I'll do them later," Alex shouted from the dining room. I walk in right as she rolls her eyes at Alex and returns to doing the dishes. I heard Alex mumble brat under his breath, and I chuckled and shook my head as I kept walking.

"Do you need help?" I ask as I walk up to Olivia and hug her from behind. I can't help it. I just want to touch her all the time. I can't seem to top myself. Olivia looks over her shoulder and smiles at me. "No, I got it, beautiful. Go relax, and I'll be there in a minute."

Beautiful.... Hmmm.... I haven't been called beautiful in so long that it sounds weird. But coming from her mouth, it sounds so confident and final that it's impossible to argue with her.

I walk back into the living room and sit on the sofa near the fireplace. Alex walks back and forth from the table to the sink, cleaning up after dinner. I'm not used to sitting down when cleaning needs to be done. Andrew would have screamed at me and probably beat the shit out of me if I had been sitting and he had been the one who had to clean. He was a firm believer in the old tradition that women should be the ones to serve men, do all the cooking and cleaning.

I don't even understand how that relationship went downhill so fast, from a good night at the bar to me becoming a murderer. I still haven't told Alex what happened. I plan to keep it that way, but his questions are becoming more persistent. I have a terrible feeling that he knows something is up and will put the pieces together sooner or later. I will have to handle that when that happens, but until then, I'm not saying anything.

I am sitting in the bar, sipping a whiskey sour, watching the NHL game on the TV. I don't know much about hockey, but I know they look damn good playing it. I pick at the fries that are in the basket next to me. A red-headed man sits beside me, ordering a Bud Light, then swivels to watch the TV. I admire him from the side without trying to make it too noticeable. He is fit; his black shirt is snug around his biceps, and he is wearing a red hat with the college team logo, I think, but I'm not sure which one. I don't follow sports. They have never been my thing. To be honest, they are boring to watch, in my opinion.

I tried cheerleading when I was ten years old, but I wasn't coordinated enough to dance, let alone stand on someone's shoulders in the air. Being petite made me a perfect candidate for a flyer. The coach was so excited to get me up in the air. She had them throwing me, trying to get me to do flips in the air—absolutely not. That was the scariest time of my life. I shake my head out of my memory.

"Can I have another whiskey sour, please?" I ask, raising my glass for the bartender. This gets the attention of the guy sitting next to me.

"Put her whiskey sour on my tab." He says in a deep, growly voice. I look over at him and smile. "Thanks, you didn't have to do that for me."

"I would do anything for a pretty girl like you." He gives me a crooked smile.

I can't help but brush my hair behind my ear and smile at him. He was charming and funny. We had a great time talking all night until the last call was made. He walked me to my car and gave me his number.

I get pulled out of my memory when Alex plops beside me on the couch, making me bounce off the cushion. "What are you thinking about, beautiful?"

"Just how different I pictured my life five years ago." I start biting my nails, waiting for Alex to say something. He just smiles up at me without a question in his eyes. It is one of the many things I admire about him. He knows something is going on in my head, but he also gives me my space, so I can approach him when I'm ready.

"Well, I hope it has turned out better than you planned five years ago." He chuckles, and Olivia walks in.

"What did I miss?" She singsongs as she walks over to the little loveseat to my left.

"I was daydreaming, and Alex was asking how differ-ent life is now than how I planned it five years ago."

"Hopefully, different in a good way. I know my life is completely different from what I planned, but in the best way possible," She smiles at me with a million-dollar smile. I feel starstruck as I stare at her. She is absolutely gorgeous, and I don't think she fully realizes it.

"I got an idea!" Alex jumped up from his seat on the couch, jumping around like a kid in a toy store. I swear this grown man has more energy than I would know what to do with.

"What's your plan, hot stuff?" Olivia says in a sassy tone. She is calm and collected, with the perfect amount of sass. I wish I could do that, but I am too afraid to step on toes. I guess that's what I was brainwashed to feel for the last five years. Alex has never made me feel that way.

"Truth or dare!" Alex screams. I rub my ears from him, yelling into them.

"Can you not make me have hearing loss, please?" I joke with him as he rolls his eyes at me.

"What are we, twelve?" Olivia said as she crossed her arms.

"I sure hope you aren't twelve, for what I have planned for you." Alex winks at her, and she sticks her tongue out at him.

They playfully bicker back and forth for a minute before Olivia gives in. "Fine! We can play truth or dare, but don't do anything stupid for dares." Alex pumps his fist in the air with a mumble of the word yes under his breath. He does a little victory dance, then sits back in the chair to my right.

"Ok, since Olivia wants to set boundaries for how we play, she should go first." Alex shines his best shit-eating grin her way and starts to rub his hand like he is a mastermind with an idea.

"Bet! I got this!" She sweeps her hair off her shoulder and looks around the room, stopping on both of us for a second longer than anything else, a glimmer of heat and mischief showing in her eyes.

"Alex! Truth or dare?" She is challenging him.

"Dare. Obviously!" He rolls his eyes at her. These two are freaking adorable together. Honestly, I feel like I don't belong in the mix at all. They are flirty and playful, and I feel like I should be hiding in a corner.

"I dare you to kiss Rachel. And not just a peck. Kiss her like you mean it! I see the way you can't keep your eyes off of her. You want her! And matchmaker Olivia is on the job!" She looks at me and winks. I can guarantee that my face is beet-red right now!

Alex gets up from his seat, walks over to me, and holds his hand for me. I hesitate for a moment, then finally place mine in his. He pulls me up to stand in front of him. My little five-foot-nothing self looks like an elf compared to his gigantic self. I look up into his eyes, and those big brown eyes twinkle with what looks like want. I give a quick nod to tell him to get on with it.

That is all the permission he needs before he grabs the back of my neck and smashes his lips into mine. I swear I see stars and feel electricity tingling all over my body, and wet pooling in between my legs. This man is one hell of a kisser, and I don't want him to ever stop kissing me.

Chapter Twenty-Five

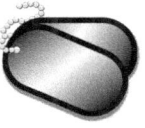

Alex

I knew my lips would always find their way back to Rachel. She is like a magnet that I never want to break apart from. I grab the back of her head, tangle my hands into her soft, straight, blonde hair, and pull her closer to deepen the kiss. I am rewarded with a small moan from her lips. That small moan changes something in me; it turns me completely feral. I growl into her mouth and push my ever-growing hard length into her stomach. She backed up a step, where the back of her legs were against the couch. I slowly push her shoulders down to lower her onto the couch. When she is finally seated, I give her one last peck on the lips, stand up, and turn.

I face Olivia, who is sitting on the loveseat with lust-filled eyes that are begging for more to happen. I reach out my hand to her, and she hesitates, turning to look at Rachel. Rachel nodded quickly, giving Olivia the reassurance she needed. She looked as if she was just as anxious to see what would happen as I was. When

Olivia finally grabbed my hand and stood up, I wrapped her in a hug. Putting two fingers under her chin, I tilt her head slightly to make her look me in the eyes.

"I want you, Olivia," I say with so much confidence that it's final. Olivia nodded, and I fused my lips with hers.

She pulls back just enough to whisper against my lips, "I am yours.", then returns to the kiss.

When I thought my cock couldn't get any harder—now it's hard as steel. Rubbing up against her stomach like I did with Rachel, trying to get some friction and hopefully ease the pressure in my pants. These girls have me wound up as tight as a spring, ready to be set free. One move from either of them, and I will combust.

Olivia puts her hand on my chest to push me back slightly, making a small gap between us, and smiles at me. Her red hair falls perfectly around her face, and her freckles along her nose and cheekbones are on full display since she only has eye makeup on, none of that stupid face-covering shit. She doesn't know this, but I prefer her natural beauty better than all that shit caked onto her face. I have never been a fan of women wearing makeup. I love natural beauty, and both of my girls are as beautiful as they come.

She slightly steps out of my grip and reaches out her hand toward Rachel, inviting her into our embrace. Rachel hesitates at first, but Olivia doesn't give her a second to overthink this. She grabs Rachel's hand, pulls her between us, pushes Rachel into my chest, and moves her face up to look at mine. It seems like Rachel is in shock about what is happening, so Olivia continues to move her like a doll. I would be lying if I said it didn't turn me on to watch these two beautiful women together. Olivia is more dominant, and Rachel is more submissive, the perfect yin and yang.

Rachel looks up at me with big blue eyes and a shy smile, grabs my neck, and kisses me deeply—my tongue seeking entrance into her mouth. Wanting to taste everything, she is willing to give. I reach behind Rachel, grab Olivia, and pull her towards me, pushing the two girls together as I devour Rachel. I can see Olivia start to kiss down the side of Rachel's neck, causing Rachel to push into me harder. Olivia reaches between Rachel and me, grabs my cock through my jeans, and gives it a slight squeeze. I thrust my hips forward into Olivia's grip more and growl into Rachel's mouth. I can feel Olivia move her other hand up to grab Rachel's breast and squeeze it while still stroking my cock through my pants. If she keeps this up, I might cum in my pants. Her hand feels fantastic on me. I reach around and grab Olivia's ass and squeeze it tight while spreading her cheeks through her dress. She has such a perfect ass. I could grab it all day and never get tired of it. Rachel is between us, allowing Olivia to explore her body while I take control of her mouth.

Rachel moves her hands, exploring my chest with her hands, sliding them under my shirt and over my abs.

She removes her mouth from mine. "Kiss her."

I look over at Olivia, who is still exploring every inch of Rachel as if trying to memorize every curve of her body with her hands. I grab Olivia's face, bring it to mine, and kiss her deeply. I hear Rachel's breath hitch when she sees us kiss. Olivia breaks off the kiss with a smile and pulls me into Rachel more, bringing the three of us as close as possible.

Chapter Twenty-Six

Olivia

I didn't plan for today to go this way, but I'm not mad about it. I have a beautiful woman in the middle of myself and a sexy ass man to make a sexy ass human sandwich. I reach up and gently move Rachel's hair over her left shoulder. I give a small kiss on her shoulder where the strap of her silver dress falls. The contact of my lips to her shoulders sends a shiver down her back, and goosebumps cover her arms.

She starts to wiggle between Alex and I, causing her juicy ass to rub all over me while her hands trace over Alex's body. I don't blame her because his body is delicious. Her constant rubbing on me is making me want her even more. I have never wanted someone as much as I wish Rachel and Alex. Yes, I want both of them. Right now!

I walk them to the couch and slowly push Alex down, making him lie on his back. I then guide Rachel to straddle his chest. I straddle Alex's hips behind Rachel and continue my kisses of torture up her neck to her ear. I start to nibble on her ear, and she giggles and tries to move away from me. That sound is pure magic. I have never heard a cute giggle before. I want to make that giggle a permanent sound in my life. I wish I could record it and save it for later.

I grab her and bring her closer to my chest and start to rub my hands down Rachel's sides and grab her ass in my hands, massaging them lightly, and she leans back on my shoulder, letting out a sigh of contentment. I see Alex's hands roaming up her thigh towards her black lace panties, which we can now see because her dress is scrunched up on her hips. He stops before actually getting to her pussy and looks at her with an arched eyebrow asking for permission. I completely understand after all she has been through. I would never not ask for permission.

With labored breaths, she leans over and grabs Alex by the throat, aggressively telling him, "Don't you dare stop now, you tease!"

I laugh and turn her head towards mine, devouring her in a deep kiss. Her lips are so soft, like fluffy clouds that I never want to break apart from. It has been a while since I have kissed a girl–no, a woman– and I don't remember it being this captivating, never this soft, and absolutely never this electrifying. It's as if Rachel's lips are a drug, and I am the junkie who can't get enough. I would gladly be addicted to Rachel if she would let me. I have a feeling her lips are not going to be the only thing I get addicted to.

I work my hands under her shirt, up to her perky, perfect breasts, and start giving them both attention through her bra, causing her nipples to harden and poke through her bra.

I lean into her and whisper in her ear. "Do you want me to keep going?"

"P–please don't stop. Feels so good." She whines to me.

"Your wish is my command, princess." I look at Alex, who has a knowing expression. I nod and get off his lap. He lifts Rachel, places her on the couch, and then stands. She lets out a frustrated whine, crosses her arms, pouts like a 2-year-old who is not getting her way, and looks up at us with the cutest puppy dog eyes I have ever seen. I couldn't help but laugh at the way she was acting. Little does she know that we are about to take the absolute best care of her.

Alex and I work our way out of our clothes as fast as humanly possible, and when we are both completely naked, our eyes, full of hunger, land on Rachel. We turn to stalk towards her, and she pulls her legs into her chest and squeals in excitement. I lift her into my arms and carry her up the stairs toward where I assume the bedrooms are. I have never been to Alex's house, so this is a hide–and–seek game to find a bed.

I use my foot to kick open the first door to the left when I get to the top of the stairs, and sigh in relief when I see the master suite through the doorway. I stalk into the room with Alex on my heels. I don't think he has taken in the fact that I just carried Rachel up the stairs, but in reality, I have carried heavier drunk fuckers before, and she weighs nothing.

"Olivia! Put me down! I'm too heavy." Rachel smacks my chest playfully, making my nipples hard, poking her in the side. Her pupils dilated, and her eyes went wide with wonder and anticipation. "Princess, you are not heavy, and I don't want to hear you say that again," I growl at her. Too heavy? You have got to be fucking kidding me.

I toss her into the air, and she lands on the bed in the center of the large room. I smile at her and see excitement in her eyes. I walk towards her, taking in every inch of her body while I can, because soon I won't be able to see all of her because I will be occupied eating my dessert. When I get to the edge of the bed, I grab her ankles and pull her toward me, lifting her into a sitting position, with Alex watching us from across the room, stroking his cock so slow it looks uncomfortable. I reach for the bottom of Rachel's dress and pull it over her head. Kissing every inch of open skin as the dress is removed, I undo her bra and slide it down her arms, then reach to cup her full breasts in my hands, loving the way the weight and softness feel so perfect.

I take a step back to admire her beauty, and she wraps her arms around her knees so no one can see her. I assume it's a reaction to all she has been through, but I want her to know how beautiful she truly is. I can't wait to worship every inch of her body until I know it better than she does. I want to be able to map out every mark on her body.

Alex approaches her, crouches down to be at eye level with her, and lifts her chin. "Don't hide from us, Muñeca. We won't do anything you don't want to do. You let us know when to stop, and we will. Pinky Promise." He holds out his pinky to her, and she gives him a half smile and grabs his pinky with her own. Then they kiss their own thumbs and press them to each other's.

Well, that was adorable.

"Ok." She nods. "I trust you." She looks around the room like she is waiting for someone to come out and attack.

My mouth falls open. Andrew! That fucker! He did a fucking number on her, and I will make him fucking pay for that. I will end him!

I walk up to Rachel, look her in the eyes, and speak from my heart. "I promise I will never let anything happen to you again. I wish I had been able to stop him earlier. You deserve nothing but to be worshipped. I can't tell you that I know what you have been through, but I can tell you I am here for you. No matter what, Princess, I will be here by your side from this day forward. I will always protect you. You have nothing to worry about."

Chapter Twenty-Seven

Rachel

Olivia grabs my chin, lifting my head to kiss me before turning her head to kiss Alex.

"Alright, princess. Are you ready for me to show you how a bi girl worships her women?" she says with a wicked glimmer in her eyes.

Um, what? What does she mean by to worship me? I swear my brain glitches out, and I can't think straight. I have never done anything with a girl. I have never even looked at a girl in a sexual way. The way I see Olivia is a whole new world to me. I don't understand my feelings. I am not sure if I can do this. Then, a thought stops me from building panic; this may be different than what I am used to, but maybe this will be different in the best possible way. In a way, I never knew I needed it. I gathered up the courage I didn't think I had and gave her a nod as a response.

She puts her hand on my chest, pushes me down slowly, and spreads my legs apart to step in between them.

I feel so exposed, even though my panties are still on. I would be lying if I didn't say it turned me on. She looks me up and down like the rarest and most precious gem she has ever seen.

She leans in, kissing me passionately, then starts peppering kisses south toward my aching pussy. I feel a jolt of electricity running through my body with every kiss she gives. I turn my head and look to the right, and I see Alex still there, just stroking himself. I lift one finger and wiggle it, signaling him to come here. Alex walks over and bends down. I grab his head, tangle my fingers in his short brown hair, pull him toward me, and kiss him as deeply as possible.

I feel Olivia kissing down my stomach; she swirls her tongue in my belly button and licks down to my pubic bone. Good God, this feels amazing. With her tongue everywhere and Alex's kisses, I can't even think straight anymore. I must be pleasure drunk if that is a real thing.

"Don't stop, Olivia," I mumble before Alex continues to fuck my mouth with his tongue. Holy shit, my body is on fire. I feel like I am about to explode. I had never felt this feeling before. My body is in overdrive; all I can do is embrace it.

Olivia finally makes it to my pussy, she proceeds to lick up my seam through my panties, and I can't help the groan in irritation. She looks up at me and smiles. She knows the torture she is causing me, and she finds it fucking amusing. She feels so good, but I want it all. I want to feel her with my panties off. Her mouth was on me, devouring me.

I start to wiggle around, looking like a needy whore as I reach down, trying to get my panties off, and I don't even care. Olivia stops what she is doing and grabs my hands. She holds them on my chest so I can't move them. I am growing increasingly impatient by the torturous second.

I finally feel Olivia release my hands as she moves her hands to my panties, wrapping her fingers around the waistband of my panties and slowly pulling them down, kissing my legs all the way down to my ankles, causing me to squirm even more with every kiss.

"Is this what you want, princess?" She says in her sexy, needy, husky voice.

"No, I want your face in my pussy! NOW!" I growl at her.

Olivia tsk, "So impatient, princess. How am I supposed to worship you if I am being rushed?"

Alex laughs, "The girl knows what she wants, so I would suggest you give it to her before she turns feral on your ass."

"Then I shall do as I am commanded," Olivia says, looking at me like she can see my soul. Then she winks and drops her head to my acing pussy, licking from my ass to my clit in one beautifully torturous lick. Moving her mouth with expertise, she then gives some extra attention to my clit. Licking and sucking until I am at her complete mercy.

"Oh, Fuck! Yes, Olivia! Right there!" I scream as my back arches off the bed.

I grab Alex again and bring him to me, running my tongue along the seam of his mouth, demanding entrance. I needed to taste him right now. I need his lips on mine more than air in my lungs. It doesn't take long for Alex to open up and take control. I slide my hand down his chest until I get to his cock. I grab him by the base, squeeze it, and start to move my hand up and down his length. Alex groans in my mouth as Olivia is eating my pussy like she is on death row, eating her last meal. She swirls her tongue over my clit, making it throb, feeling like it has its own pulse, and nibbles a little before she plunges her tongue into my hole. Holy fuck, this girl knows what she is doing!

"OLIVIA!" I scream at the top of my lungs as I let go of Alex and reach for Olivia's head. I push her into my pussy more; I never want her to leave this spot. Alex lifts his eyebrow at me and slowly gets off the bed. I keep my eyes on him as he walks around to the back of Olivia, who is bent over at the waist, pleasuring me. He gets on his knees and disappears between Olivia's legs. I can see her shift her weight to spread her legs further apart. I can only assume he is also about to have his dessert; it just happens to be in the form of a red-headed goddess. Fuck, I wish it was me in Alex's spot feasting on Olivia's beautiful pussy.

WOAH! Where the fuck did that thought come from? I am not into girls. Don't get me wrong, Olivia's tongue is magical, but I have never wanted to eat out another girl.

My stomach starts to flip, and I'm not sure if it's nerves or butterflies, but I push them down and remember that I need to be present in the moment.

I guess after tonight, I'm not sure if I'm into women or not. However, what I do know is that I have a deep desire to please Olivia, so I want to explore this with her, if she will let me.

I feel Olivia moving her body to ride Alex's face. Every time she pushes back onto his face, it makes her head move down on me, causing a beautiful rhythm of intimacy, and honestly, it is the hottest thing I have ever seen. Just the look of pure lust on Olivia's face makes me reach the peak of ecstasy and jump head-first into bliss. I am moaning and shaking, my thighs clenched around Olivia's head as she continues to lick me through my orgasm. This has to be the strongest orgasm I have ever had. My brain was foggy with pleasure; I couldn't form a word even if I wanted to. I am a boneless mess right now. Olivia looks up at me, wipes her face with the back of her hand, and smiles.

"So, princess, do you feel wanted?" She has a mischievous grin on her face. How the hell is she able to talk so calmly and controlled, while Alex is still between her thighs? She winks at me and then gives me one more satisfying lick to make sure she gets the rest of my release cleaned up and on her tongue.

Chapter Twenty-Eight

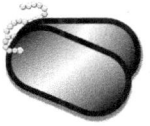

Alex

Olivia tastes so fucking good. I could be between her legs for the rest of my life and die a happy man. She tastes like sin and perfection. I see Rachel completely relax on the bed after her orgasm. That face of pure bliss she is making is perfect; I wish I had my camera to take a picture of it.

Once Olivia finished cleaning Rachel up with her tongue, she sat up, causing me to stop my feast.

"Rude!" I say to Olivia, who winks at me.

"Lie down on the bed, Alex, on your back."

"Yes, Ma'am." I give her my mock two-finger salute and lie down. I love it when she takes control. Little does she know, this is the only control she will get. Because she doesn't know the secrets I hide beneath the surface.

"Good boy," Rachel says to me with a glimmer in her eyes. I have never had a praise kink, but I could get used to her calling me her good boy. Rachel apparently isn't bothered by her past with Andrew right now because she crawled on top of me, kissed me, and then licked her way down my body. Her tongue is fucking magic.

"Holy shit, babe! Your tongue is amazing." She looks at me with so much lust in her eyes after I praise her. It seems like my little shy one also has a praise kink. I shall put a pin in that little tidbit of knowledge and address it later because I would love nothing more than to explore that kink with her.

She continues to trail her tongue down my body until she reaches my cock, raising her eyes at me with need as she circles her tongue around the tip of my cock, licking up the bead of pre-cum, and moans in approval. She continues to lick the tip until she sucks me in all the way to the back of her throat, causing my eyes to roll to the back of my head. I look over Rachel's shoulders and see Olivia staring at us like we are the best sight she has ever seen.

Rachel slowly moves up and down my shaft; she is a complete natural at sucking my cock. As she is working my dick in her mouth, she grabs my balls and rolls them in her hands. She takes my dick out of her mouth and licks from my ass to my ball sack, sucking one of my balls into her mouth and swirling it around with her tongue, then continuing to give the second one the same amount of attention. I am barely hanging on right now. I am ready to cum down her throat when she goes back to my ass and starts to lick around the ring. I have never had my ass played with before, and holy hell it feels fucking good. If she surprises me with any more secret special skills, I will be blowing my load very early, and that is the last thing I want to do.

I looked up through my hooded eyes and stared directly at Olivia. "Liv, come here!" I waved her toward me. She walked over, swiped her hair over her shoulder, bent down, and kissed me.

"What can I do for you, handsome?" She says with mischief in her voice. I grab one of her nipples and pull it hard, causing her to hiss.

"Ride my face, babe!" She looks at me with a question in her expression. She shakes whatever question she has out of her head, swings her leg over my chest, and sits down. I grab her hips to pull her toward my face. She looks at me with worry.

"Go, we got you now. It's your turn for us to make you feel good." I can hear Rachel whisper to her. Olivia nods and moves closer to my face, still with an uneasy look on her face.

"Why are you so nervous? We won't do this if you don't want to do it. That rule applies to both of you. " I raise an eyebrow at her. I don't know what trauma her past has, the way I know Rachel's, but I don't want to make her feel uncomfortable.

"No! No, no, no. I just... Ummm, it didn't end well the last time I did this. Ever since, I have been the one on the bottom." Her cheeks flushed with embarrassment. I am curious about what happened, but right now, I want to be present with my girls.

"Hey, don't be embarrassed. We will only do what you are comfortable with. As you told Rachel, we don't do anything anyone isn't comfortable with." You can physically see her shoulders releasing tension, and she nods at me. Slowly making her way up to my face. She hovers over my face but does not sit.

"Olivia, Sit!" I command

"I am not a fucking dog!" She yells back at me.

"Then do as your told and sit the fuck down on my face! Don't hover; smother me with your sweet pussy! If I die by suffocation of your cunt, I will die a happy man. Let me eat my fucking dessert."

She finally sits down enough that I can grab her hips and bring her further down. I slide my nose through her warm heat and inhale the musky scent that is all Olivia. As soon as I get my tongue to Olivia, I feel Rachel's mouth come off my dick, and she shifts on the bed.

I feel her straddle me, and in a few short minutes, Rachel fully penetrates herself with my cock. The sensation of both of my girls on me is world-altering. I don't even know how to think straight; there is so much happening right now, so I lie back and embrace the feeling of both of them on me.

I know I won't last long with these two beauties riding me, but I have no shame in finishing fast, as long as they finish also.

Olivia tries to get up from my face and shifts around. I grab her by the hips to stop her from leaving. "What are you doing?"

She doesn't answer; she just turns around to face Rachel, still hovering over my face. There is enough space that I can see Rachel on top of me, bouncing on my cock. Olivia grabs Rachel's face, bringing their lips together in a passionate kiss. It then turns to the sexiest make-out session I have ever been a part of, and I am just a spectator.

Olivia gets caught up in Rachel, and I use that to my advantage, grabbing Olivia's hips and bringing her beautiful pussy back down to my face where it belongs. I plunge my tongue into her tight cunt and feel her clench with the intrusion. When I don't let up, she finally re-laxes and starts to grind against my face, chasing the friction on her clit.

As I continue to work her pussy, I hear her breathing start getting fast and choppy. I can tell she is getting close to finishing. So, I reach up, press two of my fingers into her core, and curl them to hit that perfect spot, causing her to fall off the edge.

"ALEXXXX!" Olivia screams at the top of her lungs. Thank god the neighbors aren't close enough to hear her because these screams are for me and Rachel only!

Olivia falls back against the wall to catch her breath after her orgasm. One down, one to go.

I reach out to Rachel and grab her hips, thrusting up into her with brutal force. She moans loudly when I continue to pound into her. I can feel her smooth walls start to clamp down on my length.

Fuck! I am not wearing a condom. This is not good. I am going to have to pull out. I don't know how much longer I will last.

"I have been on birth control since my miscarriage. Stop overthinking it and just cum in me; I need to feel all of you, Alex." Rachel tells me in a breathy whisper as she bounces up and down on me like her life depends on it. As soon as I got her permission, I gave her three more powerful thrusts, and she came undone all over me. I followed suit right after, blowing all of my seed into her tight canal, and then Rachel fell on top of Olivia in a pile of sex-induced, post-orgasmic bliss.

Olivia grabs Rachel, starts stroking her hair, and kisses her head. Whispering something into her hair that only they could hear. I'm watching from below; honestly, it's the best view in the room. Both of these beautiful women hold onto each other in a state of post-orgasmic bliss.

The girls get off of me and roll to the other side of the bed. Rachel is between Olivia and I. She faces away from me and snuggles into Olivia's arms; I move behind Rachel, snuggling into her back and draping my arm over both of the girls.

Holy Fuck. BEST. SEX. EVER.

Chapter Twenty-Nine

Olivia

The following day, I woke up and snuggled into Alex's arms. I grab my phone off the nightstand to look at the time. It's a little after 8 a.m. when I notice that Rachel isn't in bed with us.

I get up and head to the bathroom first to relieve myself and brush my teeth. Then, I grabbed a black shirt from Alex's drawer and put it over my head. It barely covers my ass, but I don't even care. Walking through the hall and down the stairs, I smell bacon, and my stomach makes a loud grumble in appreciation of the smell. When I make it down the stairs, I see Rachel also in one of Alex's shirts, which hangs down to her thighs. She has music playing as her hips swing to the rhythm.

I walk up behind her, wrap my arms around her waist, and kiss her neck. She jumps, and I can't help but chuckle at her. "Good morning, princess. How did you sleep?"

She turns around and jumps into my arms, wrapping her legs around my waist, and kisses me with so much passion it almost makes me fall over. I grab her ass and squeeze as she moans in my mouth.

"Well, that is one of the most amazing good mornings I have ever gotten," I mumble into her mouth.

She laughs and wraps her legs tighter around me, kisses me again quickly, and mutters. "I missed you."

"I was right up the stairs. You could have woken me up." Before I could get my whole thought out, she was wrapping her hands in my hair and licking at the seam of my mouth to get me to open up. When she gets the access she wants, her tongue slides against mine slowly, dancing around in passion. I grab a fistful of her hair and deepen the kiss, allowing her to dominate my mouth. I want to see what she will do; I know I'm the first girl she's ever been with, but you wouldn't guess that from how she demands my attention.

I put her ass on the counter and push her thighs open so I can step in between them. I start running my hands up her thighs and exploring her body. As I work my way up her thighs to her hips, I pull her closer to me, and she wraps her legs around me again. She tightens her legs more if I am going to disappear if she doesn't hold on to me for dear life.

I make my way to the hem of the shirt she is wearing and pull it over her head. Pleased to find she has nothing on under, I reach up and grab each of her heavy breasts in my hands and squeeze them, rolling her pebbled nipples with my finger and thumb, making her arch her back. I break off the kiss, lean my head down to the rosy bud that is hard and inviting me to play, and put it in my mouth as I massage the other one in my hand, enjoying the weight, taste, and feel of her in my mouth and hand. She moans and pushes my head towards her breasts. I switch my mouth to the other breast, licking and sucking her nipple as I massage the breast I just finished devouring. She has the most amazing tits I have ever seen.

I slide my hands down from her breast to her stomach, making my way to her exposed pussy. Running my finger through her seam, I feel how wet she is.

"You are so wet for me, Princess. It seems you did miss me quite a bit." I say as I put my finger, with her juices on it, in my mouth, swirling my tongue around the finger to savor her delicious taste on my taste buds. I can't help it when I groan in approval.

"You taste so perfect. I could eat you every day for every meal for the rest of my life and still not have enough of you." I look at her glistening pussy inviting me in to finish my meal.

I stand up, grab the hair tie off my wrist, and pull my hair up into a messy bun. Rachel looks at me with hunger as she watches my every move. I wink at her, spread her legs open again, and lean in, licking her from ass to clit. I am a girl who loves to eat ass, so any chance I get, I will show her ass as much attention as she will let me.

I start to lick and suck on her clit, as her hands start pulling at my hair as best as she can with it pulled back.

"Olivia! Yes. Please. Don't. Don't stop." She is stuttering over her words as she starts to grind on my face in search of friction; she knows that only I can give her at this moment. I am currently embracing the power of being the only one who can make her cum right now.

I reach between her legs and slide my middle finger into her wet pussy, moving my finger in and out; she starts moving her hips to match the rhythm of my finger fucking her. I add a second finger, and she arches her back with a loud moan escaping her mouth. I curl my fingers to hit her G-spot, and she bucks her hips up and screams.

"OLIVVVIIIIAAAA." When she finished screaming my name, I heard my phone ring.

Usually, I would ignore it, but it's the specific ringtone I have for work calls, and if I get a work call on a Saturday morning, something must be going on.

I look up at Rachel and kiss her forehead.

"I am so sorry. I have to take this. They wouldn't call if it weren't important. We will finish what we started as soon as I get off the phone. Plus, I think your bacon is burnt." I laugh and nod towards the bacon, which is now entirely black.

Rachel lets out a frustrated groan -not that I blame her, I would be fucking pissed- then hops off the counter to fix the bacon.

I picked up my phone and saw my investigation unit partner calling me.

"Hey, Jones, What's up?" I answer, "Hey, O'Connor, we got a hit on the Los Comos case. Can you come in?" Well fuck that's not what I expected to hear this morning.

"Yeah, give me 30 minutes, and I'll be there."

"Cool, Thanks. See you soon, " he replies. Then I hang up the phone and look at Rachel, who looks sad.

"I'm sorry, princess. I have to go to the office. We got a lead on the case I am in charge of." I kiss her quickly and head upstairs to grab a pair of sweatpants from Alex's dresser.

Since I can't fit Alex's shoes and have no others here, I put on my heels from last night. I lean down to kiss a sleeping Alex on the head when he grabs me by the waist and pulls me on top of him.

"Where do you think you are going, beautiful?" Alex says in his husky, sleepy voice. It is sexy as fuck. If I had it my way, I would stay here forever.

A giggle escaped my lips when he put his face in the crook of my neck, and his stubble tickled me. "I got called into work. Got some information on a big case I am a part of." He smiles at me, smacks my ass, and lets me get out of his grip.

"Go get them hot stuff! I'll talk to you later." He smacks my ass and rolls over and finding out that Rachel is not in bed.

"She is downstairs making breakfast," I call back as I leave the room.

When I get downstairs, I kiss Rachel again, tell her I will see her later, and head out the door. On my drive to the office, I think about our great night and all the fears I overcame with two people I barely knew. It was mind–blowing in numerous ways.

When I arrive at the office, I rush into the locker room to change into my spare uniform, that I keep in my locker. I always keep a spare in case things get messy, but this situation also works. I take off Alex's clothes and my heels and start to put on my pants when Jones runs into the female locker room like his ass is on fire.

"Dude! What the fuck! Get out! I am trying to get dressed!" I screamed at him.

He just stares at me like a teenager seeing boobs for the first time in his life. Then, he looks my body up and down before he realizes what he is doing.

"Ummmm, WOW!" That's all that came out of his mouth.

"GET OUT!" I scream again and point towards the door because, apparently, he doesn't know how to listen the first time. If this is the start of my day, I am in for some deep shit.

I don't know why Jones seeing me in my bra was such a big deal. I am usually confident in what I have to offer. But it felt wrong having someone else see me so vulnerable. But I have to work with this man, so I must shake off this feeling quickly.

After getting dressed, I head to my desk. I look at my whiteboard and see all the different hits we've received on the Los Comos case. Until today, every single lead has led to a dead end. Now, I am staring at my board, trying to piece together what Jones has found, since we are the two primary officers on the case.

"They have been getting shipments out of LA." He said with a for-sure tone. I turned and looked at him as if he were stupid. We already knew that. What makes this information new?

"I had a suspicion they were. I gathered that they have multiple locations in LA and are working up the West Coast. We need to find out who they are working with to cut their roots and kill the core," I say as I use a red marker to circle the docks in LA.

"My intel tells me a shipment is coming between 9 pm and 2 am tonight. Should we do a stakeout?" Jones asks me. I am still not used to being the one in charge. "Um, yeah. Let's do a stakeout tonight. The sooner we get more intel, the better. They have been crawling underground for too long. It's time to squish these cockroaches."

Jones nods at me and returns to his desk to grab his things. We are both headed home to pack up for tonight.

"We are not sure how long we will be sitting there, so make sure you pack enough water and food. I doubt any restaurants will be open at that time." I say over my shoulder as I pack up the stuff I need from my desk for tonight.

"Also! Jones! Don't come into the locker room again without knocking." I say to him in a stern mom's voice. I'm not a mom, but it makes these fuckers in the office listen more.

"Yes, I am sorry about that. I didn't realize you had come in. And.. I heard noises, so I... uh... was checking it out. It won't happen again, I promise. " He stutters out in one breath. You can tell he is uncomfortable. I didn't mean to make him feel that way, but I don't appreciate being walked in on while changing.

"Alright, thank you for your apology. Let's grab the shit mobile, go home, grab stuff for tonight, and head out." Jones nodded in understanding before turning around and leaving the office. The shit mobile is an ugly faded blue 1994 honda accord that is the company car for stakeouts, so we don't stick out like a sore thumb.

I go to the lock box and grab the keys for the shit mobile, head out into the parking lot, and head for my house.

Once I have grabbed my to-go bag out of my closet- which is a duffle bag packed with extra underwear, a spare set of clothes, toiletries, water bottles, and a fuck ton of snacks- I head into the kitchen to grab more snacks for my bag, because I get hungry while sitting there waiting for someone to do something that will allow me to spring into action. I hate doing stakeouts; I sit in the car and do nothing for hours, and usually, there is awkward silence. I hope tonight's lead will help us make further progress with Los Comos. I am tired of chasing these fuckers in circles.

I head out of the house with my bag slung over my shoulder and head to the shit mobile. I get in the car, it starts up, and I shift into gear. I head to Jones' house to pick him up, and then we are off—a two-hour drive to the Los Angeles cargo port.

The drive was tolerable; Jones played the music, and it was actually good. Most of the time, rock music was playing. If any song I knew came on, I was dancing and singing at the top of my lungs, with Jones joining me in the Shit Mobile Concert. It was fun to goof around, even if we were on a stakeout and looking to destroy the biggest cartel in the Southwest.

I never realized how much fun Jones and I could have; usually, when we're in the office, he's shy and to himself, unless he runs into the girls' locker room, apparently.

We pull up to the dock, and it's eerily quiet, like in movies where it's quiet, then the killer comes out and cuts everyone's throats. Jones looks around. His gun is already in his lap, ready for any sign of trouble. But there is no one here. We parked where the workers parked to make it less obvious that a car was randomly on the dock, but to our surprise, there weren't many cars out here tonight.

We walked to where the cargo ships were typically moored and unloaded, but still, there was no one around. We passed by a hut that could only fit one person. It was an office-like building with a sign on the window listing what to expect today, and sure enough, it was an extremely small list, showing that they had received the last load by 9 am today. That's awfully convenient, knowing what is happening tonight. There's no way these guys weren't paid a pretty penny to let the Cartel take over the dock tonight and keep their mouths shut.

Who else would pay someone off like that besides Los Como? The question is, what cargo are they getting today? Humans? Drugs? Guns? Who knows? It could be all three, for all we know. We know they dip their toes into every underground dealing imaginable.

"Hey, let's go back to the car and get strapped up. Then, we can watch until we see any flicker of life and head back out. I am not sure what time everything is happening, but I have a gut feeling that things will happen tonight after all we saw on the dock." I whisper as I walk away. Jones just follows me like a lost puppy dog, not saying a word and trying to keep up with my pace, even though I am shorter than him.

"Hey, O'Connor?" He sounds nervous as shit right now. I just turn and lift an eyebrow at him. "What if we find women and children in the cargo containers?" He seems so nervous. Not that I blame him. I am anxious, also. This shit sucks. Trafficking is a huge deal, and I hate it with every fiber of my being. If it were just drugs and Guns, I wouldn't be nearly as mad. They don't only sell women and children, but men, also. I have read through every file given to me at least a dozen times each. I wanted to know everything about the 103 they currently have in their custody.

"If humans are in those containers, we will do what we can to rescue them. We will always do what we can." He nods in agreement.

We are putting on bulletproof vests, getting every holster we can fit on our bodies, and strapping guns everywhere. I also have knives hidden up my sleeves and in my boots. I prefer knives as my weapon of choice, but the PD doesn't agree to allow me just knives. So, I make sure to follow protocol and also add my favorites around it like an accessory.

As we strap on the last of our weapons and put on our jackets to conceal them, we see three sets of headlights approaching the dock from the left. We sit and watch the three blacked-out SUVs drive down the pier like they own the place.

Once they parked, multiple men in suits stepped out and scanned the area. I am assuming these are body-guards. I see they have a gun on their hip, but there is no telling how many they have strapped under their suit jackets. After one guy looks over his shoulder and says, "All clear."

A tall, older, Hispanic-looking man with broad shoulders, salt and pepper hair, and a short, well-trimmed salt and pepper beard, also wearing a tailored suit, gets out of the SUV. Lopez García. He looks oddly familiar, but I shake off the feeling because I have been researching this man for a while now. There is no way I wouldn't feel a sense of familiarity with a man whose face I have seen in case files a million times.

He is speaking to all the other men in suits. I can't hear what he's saying, but his hands are moving quickly, and he points to the dock where a cargo ship is pulling in, then back to the SUVs. It looks like he is giving instructions for tonight. After he stops talking, five huge, black Ford Transits pull up beside the SUVs. There are probably fifteen people on the dock now in suits. I am not sure who the guards are and who the employees are, but overall, it doesn't matter to me because they all deserve to rot in hell.

When the last Ford Transit parks, four men wearing black coveralls and black baseball caps exit each van. They walk up to Lopez García and say something quickly, then turn around and open the backs of the vans, pulling out a couple of duffel bags. They lay down a plastic tarp on the ground and start securing it to the ground with a staple gun.

"That must be where they transfer humans, the tarp for bodily fluids," Jones whispers in my ear. The thought sends a chill down my spine. The thought of human trafficking makes me queasy.

After about twenty minutes of watching, a huge cargo ship with hundreds of crates finally pulls up to the dock. The coverall-clad crew members grab the line and start mooring the cargo ship. Once everything is secure, Lopez García walks up to the ship's captain and begins to speak. We are trying to be as patient as we can. We have the windows of the Shit Mobile cracked, so we can hear anything that is audible. A crane moves and picks up a large wooden cargo box. I thought they no longer used wooden cargo boxes. As the crane sets the box onto the dock, two more men in coveralls grab pry bars and open the box. One of the men in the suits yells, "Get in line! Heads down! Shut the fuck up!" You hear crying through the commotion.

A line of boys and girls between 3 and 17 walk out of this enormous cargo box. My heart drops. There have

to be at least one hundred kids right there. None of them
are the faces I memorized from the files. These are all
new children who have been captured and brought here.
There are all races lined up here. I see an older girl,
probably around 15, comforting a smaller boy around 4.
She kneels down in front of him and grabs his face with
both hands, using her thumbs to wipe away his tears.
She then wraps her arms around him and gives him a
big hug.

One of the men in suits grabs the girl by her hair and
rips her up, causing the little boy to fall on his butt. She
holds her scalp, trying to keep her hair on her head.

"You stupid little girl! I said Stay in line and shut up!
Do you not know what that means?" He yells in her
face and jerks her head with her hair. I don't know if
she replies; all I can hear are screams from the other
kids. He then pulls her out of the line of kids and throws
her onto the dock. She hits the ground hard, causing her
head to bounce off the concrete. She doesn't move after
that. One of the coverall guys comes over, picks her up,
and puts her in one of the vans.

After they get the girl into the van, the next line comes
out of the cargo containers. This line includes adults,
men, and women of all ages and races. They line up,
looking completely out of it, as if they are drugged with
something; it is logical to get this many adults to comply.

"Hey, Jones?" I say without looking away from the
people lined up. "We need to come up with a better plan.
We can't risk these people getting caught in the cross-

fire." He nods in agreement. We need to come up with a better plan now.

We are hiding behind the closest metal cargo container from the chaos. I am twisting my silencer onto my 9mm and getting into position. I check my surroundings to make sure no one is around me as I aim at the suit closest to us. One squeeze of the trigger, and the bullet goes through his head. The suit drops with a thud, and I take aim at the next suit. Jones is behind the container next to mine, also shooting. The suits are dropping like flies; no one has noticed so far because they are too worried about their cargo. We want to take out as many suits as possible before notifying Lopez García. It will make saving these people easier if there are less people on our asses.

We shoot about eight suits before Lopez García notices some of his guys are missing.

"Someone is here! Spread out and find them!"

Jones and I turn toward the back of the pier and run as quietly as possible to the farthest back container. When I hear a shot ring out, I cover my head for any debris to come flying at me.

"Jones! We have to pick up the pace!" I yell over my shoulder. I hear his boots behind me as we run towards the back of the dock.

Five more shots ring out; all I can do is keep running.

Another shot rings out, and I hear a loud thud on the ground. I take a split second to turn my head and see Jones on the ground, blood coming out of his head. I trip when I turn back around. When I finally regain my balance, I continue to run as fast as my legs will take me.

FUCK!

Now, I am on my own. I can hear the pounding of steps behind me. My heart races as I swerve around cargo crates, trying to dodge the suits. I don't know where I'm going or what I'm doing. I am just running. If I don't, I will be shot next, and no one will save those poor people. That is the thought that keeps me going. Keeps me running.

As I round the next corner, I run straight into a broad chest in a black suit. The impact of his chest makes me fall backward.

FUCK!

He wraps his big ass arms around me, and I go to fight him off. Unfortunately, he easily has a hundred pounds on me and is at least a foot taller, if not more. I am kicking, scratching, biting, and wiggling, doing anything I can to get out of this man's grip. I have to keep running.

He puts his hands up to his ears and talks into a microphone I didn't know was there.

"I caught the redhead," he said in a growly voice.

Fuck what am I going to do now? He picks me up and throws me over his shoulder. I bang on his back and try to bite him, since that's all I can seem to do because he has a death grip on my legs. I guess this is how Fiona felt when Shrek picked her up. The only difference is that she wasn't being hauled off to her death.

We walk to the dock where everyone else is. He sets me down and grabs my wrists. I blink a few times to adjust to being back right side up, and I look straight into the brown eyes of the Drug Lord himself.

"Cuff her and put her in the SUV. Don't kill her!" He barks his orders before turning around and paying attention to his shipment again.

Before I was put into the SUV, I saw at least fifteen wooden cargo crates containing people of all ages, races, and genders. I also took a quick glance at the people standing in line, being evaluated by suits. All of them were taken from their homes, and they need me, and I can't do shit because my dumb ass got caught.

My arms are handcuffed behind me, and I am placed inside the second row of the blacked-out SUV. A burlap sack is placed over my head; it is itchy and smells terrible. I can barely breathe through the material, which causes me to panic. I have to remember to calm myself down, or else I will have an anxiety attack and pass out. I need to be as focused as possible. I feel a pinch in my arm, then a burning sensation of something being put into my arm. Then, the world goes black.

Chapter Thirty

Alex

I woke up at 9 a.m., and Olivia was gone. I remember she got called into work. Rachel wasn't in bed either; Olivia was saying something about Rachel cooking breakfast. I got out of bed and went to the bathroom. When I got back into the room, I put on grey sweatpants, grabbed my phone, and headed to the kitchen for coffee.

I walk down the stairs and see Rachel on the couch with her glasses on, reading a book. I love it when she wears her glasses. She looks so cute with them on.

"Good Morning," she says from the couch, wrapped up in a blanket, not looking up from her book. I walk up to her, grab her face with both hands, and fuse my lips to hers. Once I step back, I whisper, "Morning, beautiful. How did you sleep?"

"Better than I have in ages." She looks up at me through her dark lashes. I can get used to this kind of wake-up call every morning; the only thing that would make this morning better would be Olivia being here.

I check my phone as the coffee is poured into my cup from my fancy coffee machine. I don't have any missed calls or texts from Olivia. I shoot off a quick text to her, just letting her know that I am thinking about her because apparently I turned into a pussy whipped sapp with these women, but I have no shame in it! I will wear that title with a badge of honor because I am getting double the pussy.

> Me: Hey, I miss you! Hope the case is going good. Call me or text me when you get the chance. I will be home all day with Rachel, and we will be waiting for your return :)

I grab my coffee and sit next to Rachel on the couch. I went through the other texts from Smith and some of the other guys. Smith is bitching about not getting laid last night, James is bitching about being hungover, and as I keep reading, I notice that it is all bitching. My mind goes back to last night and all the fun we had. I can't relate to any of these guys; I have nothing to bitch about besides maybe that I wish Olivia were here today with Rachel and me.

It's nice out today. Maybe I can convince Rachel to get on the back of my bike. I'm not sure if she's into motorcycles or not, but I think it would be sexy to have her holding onto me for dear life while the world passes us by. Shit, maybe I can take her to my hometown and to the beach, where I used to go as a kid until we hear back from Livy.

When I make it to the couch, Rachel comes into view, and my breath catches in my throat. She is fucking gorgeous! Her hair is in every direction, and she is wearing my black undershirt that hangs down to her mid-thigh. She looks up at me again and smiles. "Thank you for last night, by the way."

"The honor was all mine, beautiful. So, I was thinking that if you're up for it, we could go on an adventure today. How does that sound?" She looks around, worried.

"What if Olivia comes back and we are not here?" She says in a panic.

I can see her little brain going into panic mode. I need to shut this down before she blames herself for something that has been taken out of context. "Shhh, I texted her and told her we were waiting for her to come home and to text us when she got off. When she is off, we will come back home and be here waiting for her." Her eyes go big, and her eyebrows rise with the ending of the sentence. Fuck! Well, how do I fix this word vomit?

"What I mean is..." She puts her finger to my lips to shush me and says, " She feels like home. I know this is all new, and it's only been one night, but I could tell last night that I was home with both of you by my side. I haven't ever felt that way; it is new and scary, but I am willing to be open-minded." She stole my breath with that speech. Holy fuck, how did I get so lucky to find this angel?

She grabs her coffee cup, walks into the kitchen to start the coffee machine, and turns back to me. "So, um. Last night was the first night I ever did anything with a woman. I have never kissed a woman, let alone had any sexual relationships with one. I'm not entirely sure how to feel about everything. I also don't know how to explain my feelings for Olivia." She sounded embarrassed and shy, but her eyes told a different story, with lust burning in them.

"And? What did you think?" I ask with a raised eyebrow and all the curiosity in the world, because I know it's the hottest thing I've ever seen.

"Honestly? It was fucking hot!" She says with a devilish grin. "Olivia is hot as hell and knows what she is doing. I also felt a spark when she kissed me, like electricity going through my body, bringing me to life. I felt the same spark this morning when we were having sex. I am trying not to overthink things, though. After what happened with Andrew, I don't want to get my hopes up for anything." You could see her eyes fall by the end of what she was saying, and it broke my heart. This beautiful woman has been through hell and back, and there is nothing I can do about it.

"Wait a minute. You two had sex this morning and didn't think to wake me up?" I say, and put my hand on my chest to pretend to be hurt. She rolls her eyes at me and then returns to her book.

"So! I have a whole day planned for us. Are you up for it?" I say this with as much enthusiasm as I have in me.

She looks up from her book at me and nods. You can see the smile in her eyes.

"It will involve riding my bike. Are you ok with being on the back of my motorcycle?" Her eyes light up even more at that!

"That sounds like a blast!" She exclaims and jumps up from the couch.

"Alright, let's go shower, and we will get ready to go," I say. She runs to the guest bedroom across the hall, and I follow her. She must have misunderstood me when I said to take a shower. I absolutely meant together. Now that I have had her naked in my arms, I plan to be that way as much as humanly possible.

I walk into her bathroom, which is already full of steam. Rachel is humming a pop song while undressing, completely focused on her music, so she doesn't hear me come in behind her. She stepped into the shower and immediately tilted her head back to let the water run through her hair, sighing with contentment.

I take off my grey sweatpants and open the door to the shower. As I step in, I stare at Rachel under the water, eyes closed, in a completely perfect state of calm. It is one of the most beautiful sights I have seen. I have never seen her this calm, and I love it. Her life has been too crazy; that calm looks good on her. I come up behind her and wrap my arms around her body, and she jumps, and her body tenses.

"I'm sorry. I didn't mean to scare you, Muñeca," a small half-smile creeping on my lips. I felt terrible about scaring her, but I had to take a shower with her. I just want to touch her all the time.

"What were you thinking about?" I ask while I help her lather the shampoo in her hair, giving her a scalp massage while inhaling her floral scent.

"Honestly? Andrew, and how different this life is compared to the last five years I spent with him in Hell. I feel freer here, like I can breathe for once." You can see her shoulders relax after she lets everything out.

"You are safe here. Andrew can never get to you again. You need to leave him buried where he is." I say that, hoping to get her to talk about the day she left. She sighs and walks under the water stream, letting the water flow down her body.

When we go outside towards my bike, I turn to her, put the helmet I bought for her on her head, and fasten the strap. I want to make sure she is safe at all times with me. I swing my leg over my bike and start the engine. I feel the engine purr through my body, letting the feeling soak deep into my bones. She climbs behind me and holds me tight like a good little backpack, and I roll us forward down the driveway. Once we are on the road, I start driving slowly, and she tightens her grip around my waist. When she finally loosens her grip on me, and as I feel her relax, I speed up my bike a little bit and head onto the open road.

The beach I plan to take her to is just five minutes from the house where I grew up. No one knows about it because you have to hike a little through the woods to reach it and see the beauty on the other side. I also have a nice spot to hide my bike, so no one knows when I am out here. This is my little piece of heaven that I refuse to share. Until now...

We turn off the exit and enter the small town of Morro Bay—Home Sweet Home. Traffic is light as we approach my Ma's house. I drive my bike cautiously through the streets because I have precious cargo on the back.

I finally turn toward my hiding place and slow down my bike. The ancient volcano stands tall and majestic before us. We hit the dead end of the street, where the woods start. I turn off my bike and get off. I helped Rachel get off the bike and take her helmet off, setting one helmet on each handlebar.

"Where are we?" She asks, all starry-eyed at the nature surrounding us.

"This is my thinking spot. I come here to make all my important, life-changing decisions," Pushing my bike further into the woods until we get to the perfect spot to leave it hidden. "Ok, then, where are we going?" She says as she races to catch up with me.

"Can you just let me have one single surprise for you?" I say in the most dramatic voice I can muster up. She rolls her eyes, and I swear I want to spank her for being a brat right now.

We continue our hike through the woods and finally come out onto the rocky cliff. I grab Rachel's hand and pull her to the stairs to the left that lead down to the beach. Once we get to the sand, I stop and take off my shoes, and Rachel does the same. We continue to walk towards the three large rocks that I love to sit on and stare out into the water.

"Wow. It's beautiful out here. How many people know about this place?" Rachel looked out at the waves crashing against the shore.

"I'm not sure how many people know about this place, but every time I have come out here, I have been alone." The comment apparently surprises her because her head whips towards me with her mouth hanging wide open.

"You mean to tell me you have never taken another girl out here?" The shock is evident in her voice.

"I have never taken anyone out here, ever. I never wanted to show anyone my spot. This place holds a lot of memories." This is the only place I go to be alone, so bringing Rachel here is a big deal for me. Maybe one day, we will also bring Olivia here.

I can't explain my feelings for Rachel, but they are strong and here, in my face.

I empty my pockets, putting my phone, keys, and wallet on the rock next to me. I look over at Rachel, who is staring out into the water with a small, contented smile on her face. I stalked towards her, preparing to get into the water with her.

When I reach her, I scoop her up, sling her over my shoulder, and run straight toward the water without a second thought. She starts to wiggle in my arms and squeals.

"Alex! Put me down! I am not dressed for the water!"

I ignore her protest and keep running into the water, diving headfirst. When I come to the surface, I bring her down from my shoulder and kiss her deeply and passionately. She wraps her arms and legs around me as we walk deeper into the water.

"You want to know a secret?" She whispers as if we were around a bunch of people who can't know her secret and are not alone on a secluded beach.

"Hmm?" I look at her with curious eyes. She starts to move out of my arms and swim towards the shore. I follow her, ready to bring her back out if she tries to run.

She turns towards me, takes off her shirt, and throws it on the shore. "I hate the feeling of wet clothes on my body." She eyes me as she unclasps her bra, slides it down her arms, and throws it to the shore. All I can do is watch her undress in front of me. My cock was getting hard just from watching her undress. The thought of having her again was on my mind.

She slowly and seductively takes off her pants under the water. Who knew someone could seduce you when you can't even see them taking off their clothes? She throws her pants and thong onto the shore and walks deeper into the water towards me.

She puts her hands on my chest and looks up at me. "It looks to me that you, sir, have too many clothes on." She winks at me and then dives under the water, swimming away from me. Oh, this girl is going to get it!

I get undressed as fast as I can. These damn wet clothes make it almost impossible to do anything quickly. When I finally get them off, I throw them to the shore and swim after Rachel, who is further into the ocean now. As soon as I reach her, I grab her around the waist and pull her to my chest, nibbling on her ear.

"You are such a tease, Muñeca," I whisper to her.

"No. Actually, a tease would be someone who messes with you and then leaves you to handle the blue balls they gave you. I have every intention of fucking the shit out of you." She grabs my head and pulls me down to her level to kiss me, capturing my bottom lip with her teeth. I groan in response and lift her so she is positioned over my aching cock.

Rachel reaches down in between us, grabs my cock, and lines it up with her entrance, slowly lowering herself onto me. Torturously slow. She grabs my face again and smashes her lips to mine in a battle of tongue and teeth.

I lift her and bring her back down on me with force while she makes the cutest little whimpering noises. She fucking perfectly wrapped around my cock. Is it possible to live in someone's pussy forever? Because I don't want to leave.

"Rachel! Oh my God. You feel so good, baby! I am not going to last long," I say with a ragged breath. I start to pick up speed, lifting her and bringing her down as

I thrust up into her at the same time, making sure to hit her G-spot every time.

A couple of thrusts later, she clamps down on me in a powerful orgasm as I am emptying myself into her. She wraps her arms around my neck and tries to catch her breath.

"That was amazing." She says before kissing me deeply.

I couldn't agree more.

Chapter Thirty-One

Olivia

I wake up, my head pounding, and the light is too bright. I blink, trying to get my vision to clear up, when I hear footsteps in the distance. I am tied to a chair with rope on my wrists and ankles; the room is solid concrete, muggy, and humid. I need my damn eyes to adjust so I can find a way out of here. Jones is dead; I remember that picture vividly in my head, so I am on my own now to figure this all out. But my question is, why didn't they kill me also?

I heard a key in the door lock, and the hinges creaked open. That didn't help my headache at all. When I looked up, my eyes finally began to adjust to see the big guy who had carried me to the SUV.

"Oh, look. The pig is awake." He smirks.

"You can't come up with anything more original than pig? What the fuck do you want? Why not just kill me so there is one less cop on the road?" I say, trying to get up from this chair, but failing.

The big guy leans against the door frame, laughing at me. "Boss said you were a feisty one, just like your mama. It must be the red hair." My mom? What the fuck does my mom have to do with this?

He pushes off the door frame and starts to walk back out. "I am going to let the boss know you are finally awake. He would like to speak to you."

The fuck is going on. My brain is going a thousand miles an hour, making it almost impossible to come up with a logical thought. Now, that big dude wants to say something about my mom. I swear this better be some terrible yo mama joke, or I'm gonna fucking flip out on his ass.

I have been sitting here for what feels like hours, waiting for something to happen. Anything to happen. Kill me. Don't kill me. At this point, I don't care as long as something is happening.

I dozed off for a bit and woke up to the sound of the key in the lock. I turn my head towards the door to see who the hell is finally coming in; after making me wait so damn long and sure as fucking shit, Lopez García himself steps into the room, followed by the big dude.

He turns around and shuts the door so softly that you barely hear the click of the latch.

"Hello, Olivia, " he said with an evil grin. I can't even speak; I stare at him, anger and confusion running through my blood.

"You must be wondering how I know you. Well, you see... Your father and I go way back, and we have some unfinished business to take care of. You, my dear, happen to be collateral in this unfortunate situation." Business with my dad? What was that even supposed to mean?

"My dad? What kind of business do you need with my dad? How do you even know my dad?" I am shaking from the cold room, or maybe it's because I need to pee badly. Who fucking knows anymore?

"You see, your dad made a business deal with me and then backed out after the agreement was made. So I am getting payment for the inconvenience caused by his actions." He studies his nails like a girl who just got her manicure done. "It's extremely unfortunate that you had to be brought into this little misunderstanding, but business is business."

"Dude! What the fuck are you talking about? My dad is just the president of a bank. What kind of deal would he strike with someone like you?" I spit at him, trying my hardest not to scream at him, but my blood is ready to boil over with anger. I don't allow people to talk shit about my family. And here he is, calling my dad a liar to my face. Fuck him!

"Wow! I thought August was kidding when he said you knew nothing of what he was doing. The fact that you think he is just a banker is comical. He may work physically in a bank, but dear, your father is the furthest thing from a banker."

"What the fuck are you talking about?" I screamed. I don't know what he is talking about. My dad has been the bank president since Oliver and I were born. I have gone to the bank with him multiple times. I have seen his office. A regular fucking office, with a picture of the four of us on his desk and even a leather couch.

Lopez García pulls out his phone, completely calm, which makes me even angrier. "How about we give Daddy dearest a call? Shall we?" The next thing you hear is ringing.

"García, what the fuck do you want?" You hear my father's voice on the other end, and García puts a finger to his mouth to shush me before I can say anything. I shut up because the last thing I need to do is scream and get shot. I don't see big dude hiding in the corner, but I know he at least has his hand on his gun, ready to shoot me for any little mistake I could make.

"O'Connor! So nice to hear from you. I wanted to bring the proposition I sent your way that you refused back to the table and see if you would reconsider."

"I told you. I am not going to be getting into the skin trade. It's one thing to transport guns or drugs, but I draw the line at humans," Dad sounds fucking pissed on the phone. What the fuck? Does Dad deal drugs and guns? Why the fuck didn't I know that. How has this never been brought up?

"See, I was afraid you would say that, O'Connor. But I have something of yours that might change your mind." He moves the phone towards me, "Go ahead, sweetheart, say hello to Daddy, dearest." A deep chuckle comes from his throat as he finishes his sentence.

"Um. H–Hi, Dad." I said with a stutter. I don't even know what to think or say; my whole life has been a lie, and now I am collateral in this bullshit. I do know I need to get the fuck out of this dungeon.

"OLIVIA! " My dad is completely freaking out right now. I hear something shatter in the background, and growling coming from my dad.

"Yes, Olivia is here with me. She is a pretty little thing, isn't she? She would make me so much money for the right buyer." He rubs his finger down my cheek, cupping my chin. I try to jerk my head out of his hand, and he squeezes my face tighter.

"Let her go. We will ..." My dad sounds broken and desperate, and then Lopez García cuts him off.

"You see, O'Connor. I would believe you had you not backed out once before. So, I don't trust you. Olivia will stay in my care until all the details are in motion. Don't worry; I will take extra special care of her for you." Before my father could speak, Lopez García hung up the phone and smiled at me.

"You see, sweet girl. Your daddy isn't an innocent little Bank President. I never pegged you as the ignorant type. So, either you are stupid, or your father did a good job of hiding it from you. Especially knowing your brother is his right-hand man." Oliver? Right-hand man? Why wouldn't he tell me? We don't have secrets. Well, I know I don't, but I guess I can't say the same for my twin. Who else in my life has been lying to me? My hands are shaking, my fists are so tight, my knuckles are turning white, and my teeth are grinding so hard I might chip a tooth. I am just trying to hold it together at this point, but it seems like that is a losing battle as a tear rolls down my cheek.

"Tony, please get Olivia out of the basement, clean her up, and take her to her room, " He says as he walks out the door.

Tony turns towards me with an evil grin on his face and stalks towards me. He takes his knife from his hip and cuts the rope off my wrists and ankles, replacing the rope on my wrists with handcuffs, picking me up like I weigh nothing, and throwing me over my shoulder. The contact with his shoulder to my stomach takes the breath out of my lungs. He chuckles at my wheezing sounds as I try to catch my breath and then stomps up the stairs.

Chapter Thirty-Two

Rachel

"Where the fuck have you been, Rachel? Out with some guy?" Andrew yells in my face. Spit flinging onto my face with every word he says.

"No, I texted you and told you I had to stay after class for a group project. You can check with my classmates and professor if you need to." I tell him, trying not to yell but to make sure he can hear me. Andrew's hand comes up and slaps me across the face, and I feel the sting immediately.

"I don't know who the fuck you are yelling at bitch! I own you. You owe me everything. I pay for this house. I pay for the food. If you had your way, I would probably pay for you to get a fucking boob job also, so you can go flaunt your tits around and fuck other guys!" I look at him dumbfounded.

"A boob job? Really, Andrew? First off, never once have I asked for a boob job. And you pay for the apartment because I moved in with you. It was yours before we *even got together. You told me not to worry about paying half the rent and to focus on school." My blood is boiling; don't say something stupid, Rachel. How could he even be saying shit like this?*

That's a lie... He always says something and then contradicts himself. It's a never-ending battle.

"Ok, Andrew. You're right. I'll get a job to help support us." Sass dripping like venom from my words. "Bitch I don't know who the fuck you think you are talking to..." Andrew screams as he slaps me across the face again. This time, it made me fall to the ground with the impact of the hit. I grabbed my cheek as if it would stop the stinging and realized it was wet. I realized tears were falling. I wiped them away quickly, making sure Andrew didn't see them.

"You should be grateful for what I do for you! You would be a prostitute on the side of the street without me! I made you who you are! You literally should be bowing down to me and kissing my fucking feet, you ungrateful bitch!" He continued to scream as I just lay on the ground and waited for him to finish his fit. I cock my eyebrow at him by the end of that statement. Bow down to him? Made me? What in the actual fuck?

He starts to undo the belt of his pants, and I know what is coming next. I just close my eyes and find a different place to be instead of this hell. If I fight him, I know that he will beat the shit out of me. The last time I tried to push him away, I walked away with a black eye and a broken arm. Since then, I have tried to ignore him as much as possible and keep my mouth shut so he wouldn't do this.

He pops the buttons on his pants and pulls them down without unzipping the zipper. Getting frustrated because they are not doing what he wants, he jerks them off and falls to his knees.

Grabbing his shaft, he jerks it a few times, then grabs my shorts and panties, ripping them down my legs, and thrusts in. There was no time for adjustment, no time for anything, just to feel the pain radiate through my body.

I scream out in pain from the intrusion. He reaches down and grabs my neck, squeezing as hard as he can. I claw at him, trying to get him to let go. When he feels me fighting him, he starts to shake me by my throat, causing my head to come forward and slam back down on the floor, the pounding in my head getting worse with every blow.

"You fucking want this bitch! All you want is this fucking cunt filled twenty-four fucking seven. I am doing you a fucking favor." Andrew is spitting as he is yelling. I can't help but let the tears fall down my cheeks; My vision starts to get blurry from the lack of oxygen.

"Wake up! Rachel, wake up!" I hear a voice in my subconscious. Who is saying that? That's not Andrew's voice.

My eyes fly open, my hand goes straight to my neck to rub the pain away, and I am gasping for air. Alex is above me, gently shaking my arm, trying to wake me up.

"Hey, are you ok? What's going on?" I sit up and move away from him. Terrified of the dream I was just having. I look around the room to make sure Andrew is nowhere to be found before my breathing starts to regulate.

"You were screaming and yelling at Andrew to stop. I assumed you were having a nightmare, so I woke you up. Here is some water." He hands me a glass of ice water, and I take a big gulp to soothe the heat running through my body from the nightmare. I reach up, wipe the sweat off my forehead, and try to get my breathing back to normal. My heart is racing so fast that it feels like it will jump out of my chest.

Alex sits down next to me, grabs my hand, and pulls my head to his chest. He stops right before my head is lying flat on him to make sure I am okay with what is happening. Sighing in relief, I nod and lay it on his chest. He starts to rub my hair, and the comfort it brings is unexpected but needed more than I realize.

I look up at him with tears in my eyes, "Thank you for waking me up. I was having a nightmare of Andrew raping me. You would think I would be used to..."

"Stop it!" Alex says sternly as his face turns murderous with rage, "You should never be used to being raped because some low-life piece of shit thinks he can take advantage of you! You are so much more than a hole for anyone to fuck!" All I can do is nod as the tears continue to stream down my face.

I wish I could believe his words. But that is all I was for as long as I can remember. A pretty face and a warm hole. I lay my head back down on him and just embrace his warmth.

Chapter Thirty-Three

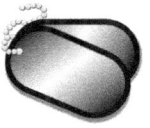

Alex

I woke up to blood-curdling screams. I have never shot up so fast in my bed ever. Rachel was kicking and screaming next to me in bed. She was sweating like crazy and hyperventilating.

Then I heard, "No, Andrew, please don't." In a soft whimper. A complete contrast to the screaming I woke up to. I have to wake her up. She doesn't deserve to live through that nightmare over and over again. Andrew is fucking dead; he shouldn't be haunting her dreams.

"Rachel, wake up. Please wake up," I say, softly shaking her arm. She stirs but doesn't wake up.

"Wake up, Rachel! Wake up!" I yell, shaking her harder. Her eyes spring open with fear.

I soothe her and talk her through the dream. The whole time she is telling me how Andrew used her and how she was nothing but a fuck toy for him. I had to keep my temper in check. My jaw ticked with anger as she kept crying into my chest. I am so pissed that she had to go through that, and there was nothing I could do. If Andrew weren't already dead, I would have him chained up in a warehouse at my mercy. I would make his death slow and painful. I would make him hurt a million times worse than he hurt Rachel. By the time I was done with him, he would be begging me for death.

I calmed Rachel down, and she fell back asleep. But I was so worked up that sleep was a thing of the past for me, given how much adrenaline ran through my body. I hit the gym I had set up in my garage to handle my anger. A little exercise should help my issues with a man who is six feet under. I wish I were the one to send him there, but the job is done.

I start off my workout with a three-mile run on the treadmill. I turn on 80s music as loud as I can. Thank god I decided to make this room soundproof. I run three miles in less than ten minutes, pushing my legs harder than ever. I want to feel the burn in my muscles; I need to be sore and unable to walk tomorrow.

After my run, I go to the bench press and lift for an hour. At this point, all of my muscles are shaking and screaming at me to stop. But I keep pushing; I have to push myself further than ever. Honestly, my mood hadn't changed by the time I finished. I am just sweaty and pissed now. This is lovely.

I walk upstairs to my room, making sure not to wake Rachel in the process. I shower, let the hot water soothe my aching muscles, and contemplate what I must do. Olivia is still not home, and I haven't gotten a single text or call from her. I am trying to think of anything I know about the San Diego Police Department and their stakeouts. Do they usually take this long? Do they have no signal? My mind starts to come up with questions that are getting absolutely absurd because my anxiety is getting into the mix. I finally wash up and get out of the shower. Wrapping a soft white towel around my waist, I head to the closet, half-ass dry off the water, and then put on a plain white T-shirt and grey sweatpants.

I head down to the living room and make a cup of coffee. I put the pod in the machine and clicked the start button. I pull out my phone and call Olivia before letting my thoughts go dark. You never know what is going on; she could just be at the office, busy with paperwork or something. I hit the call button for Olivia's name, and the phone went straight to voicemail. Well Fuck. My thoughts start to swim around my head, and none are positive.

I then checked her social media to see if she had been online.

Nothing.

I noticed a post from a guy named Oliver saying, "10 days until my twin's birthday." Hmm, I didn't know she had a brother, let alone a twin.

I pulled up his profile, and sure enough, he looked like the male version of Olivia, from the Auburn hair to the blue-green eyes. They even have the same smile. It's kinda creepy. I messaged him to ask if he had heard from Olivia recently, explaining our situation and why I was worried about her. I ended the message with my phone number so he could call me.

I click send and stare at the message, waiting for him to read it.

It is the middle of the night; there is no way this man will reply right now, but I can't tear my eyes away from that little delivered message.

Sure enough, not even ten minutes later, I saw the message change from 'delivered' to 'read,' and my phone rang.

"Hello," I say.

"Are you Alex?" He says, you can hear the no-shit attitude in his voice.

"Yeah, I am glad you called. I was wondering if you have heard from your sister. I texted her yesterday, and she hasn't opened the message, called, or done anything else since she left my house yesterday morning." I know he can hear the desperation in my voice, and I truthfully don't give a shit; I am fucking desperate.

You could hear his heavy breathing on the other end of the phone, which made my heart race even more. "No, I haven't heard from her, but I have a bad gut feeling about this. Let me call my dad to see if he has heard from her, and I will call you back." He hung up before I could reply.

Well, that didn't fucking calm my nerves. I am now panicking as I pace around the house, my hands sweating as I impatiently wait for Oliver's call. I check my phone every three seconds, as if it will magically start ringing.

As much as I want to wake Rachel up and tell her what's happening, she's had enough problems this morning with her nightmare. I do not want to cause her more stress. I'm not even sure if there s something wrong with Olivia.

My phone finally starts ringing, pulling me out of my head. I dive headfirst towards my counter to get to my phone. I slipped on the tile and had to catch myself before my face hit the counter.

"Hello," I say, completely out of breath. Fucking smooth, Alex. I smack my forehead with my palm.

"Hey, It's Oliver. I talked to my dad and have good and bad news."

"Spit it out, Oliver!" I say this a little too harshly because of the terrible scenarios running through my head at this very moment.

"Well, the good news is that Olivia is alive and okay—for now." Oliver's voice cracked slightly, and you could hear the nerves running through him.

"Okay. Oliver, please. For the love of god. Spit it out; my nerves are shot, and I can't handle half information!"

"Okay, okay. The notorious Los Como Cartel Drug Lord has her held captive." As the words come out of his mouth, my heart sinks. I feel sick to my stomach, I can't breathe, and my heart stops mid-beat.

"What do you mean, Los Como captures her?" I say as I grab the edge of the counter to steady myself. This can't be happening. What would my grandfather want with her?

"What I am saying is, Lopez García has her. He called my dad to taunt him about having Olivia because my dad refused to participate in the skin trade. My dad has refused this offer for as long as I can remember, and now he is using Olivia as leverage to get my dad to do what he wants." My mind starts to tune out what Oliver is saying, and all I can think about is that my grandfather has Olivia, and there's no telling what he's doing to her or allowing to be done to her. His stupid men are just as nasty as he is.

My mind is spinning, but one thing is absolutely clear. *Olivia is with my grandfather.*

And I will fucking get her back.

I focus on Oliver again when he says, "I am getting a plane ready to go. I will be there in five hours. Send me your address, and I will come by, and we will figure out a plan." Oliver says.

"Send me your flight information. I'll pick you up there. Before we meet, I need to make some phone calls. If this is where Olivia is, we are going to need men—lots of men. Do you have any in this area or ones you can get to come this way?" My mind is coming up with different plans and outcomes.

"Yeah, I will get them to come that way. I'll let them know what the plan is when we have one. See you in a couple of hours." Oliver hangs up the phone, and I am left to think.

Chapter Thirty-Four

Olivia

I was taken up the stairs to a room bigger than my apartment. The big guy—Tony is his name, I think—took me to the en suite bathroom and turned on the shower.

He turns and starts to reach for my shirt. "The fuck do you think you are doing, Tony? I can shower myself, thank you very fucking much, you fucking nasty bastard." He snarls at me and looks at me like I am the most disturbing thing he has ever seen.

"The boss said I need to clean you. So, shut your fucking mouth and let me do my job." He growls at me.

He pulls out a pocket knife and cuts down the front of my shirt and bra. My breast is now on full display, and he is gawking. I turn to face away from him, and he yanks my arm and spins me around so I face him again.

"I don't think so, princess. I will do as I please right now. And correct me if I am wrong, but you seem to be in no position to stop me right now."

He grabs my breast so hard that a hiss escapes my mouth. He moans as he bends down and licks from the crease between my shoulder and neck up to my ear, biting my ear so hard I can feel warm liquid trickling down my neck. This fucker just drew blood on me. I jerk my knee up, trying to catch him in his balls, but he moves out of my way too fast. I hear his deep, rumbled laugh that sends chills down my spine.

When he bends down to my ear again, he whispers gruffly, " I am going to have so much fun with my feisty new toy." Then licks my earlobe again.

I try to swing my head to head–butt him this time, but again, he steps out of my way just in time and laughs at my attempt. "Nice try, but even if you didn't miss, it still wouldn't stop me from having my fun. Now stop with all this bullshit."

He grabs his knife again, kneels down towards my legs, and wraps his arms around my thighs to make sure I don't try to kick him. He cuts down the seams of my jeans until they are cut most of the way and rips one side away with a painful tug. Then, he does the same for the other side of my jeans. The parts of the jeans that weren't cut all the way dig into my skin and leave angry red marks from his yanking.

He stands back up, walks me over to the nightstand beside the bed, pulls out some black rope, and starts to wrap it around my ankles and in between my legs so they are tight and I can't slip out. I kick and move to make it as difficult as possible, and he tsks at me, his brows scrunching together while looking up at me with a challenging look.

"Trying to make this harder for me will only make me tighten the rope more." He grabs the ropes and pulls them tight to make a point. Once he is done with my ankles, he wraps my hands with the rope behind my back, then takes the handcuffs off.

I am standing next to the bed in just my red thong and black rope now, ankles and wrists bound together.

Tony stands back up and looks at me like a master-piece he just finished, making me feel uneasy with his lingering gaze. He scoops me up and swings me over his shoulder into the bathroom, pulls down his pants and boxers, and then takes off his shirt.

I could admire his body if I weren't captured, and this guy wasn't trying to have his way with me. It seems like he puts a lot of work into it. Too bad he is a fucking psychopath.

He pushes me into the shower and quickly washes me, scrubbing me so hard it leaves my skin red and raw. Once I am cleaned to his standard, he takes me out of the shower and attempts to dry me off with a small, hard towel the size of a dish towel, leaving my hair dripping with water. He picks me up and carries me back to the bed. He undoes the rope on my wrists but quickly grabs my loose wrist and puts it above my head. I am kicking, biting, and moving, trying to get out of his grip, but all it does is make him laugh and grip my wrists tighter.

He starts to wrap the rope around the headboard. Within a second, he loses his grip on my wrist; I swing and make contact with his jaw. He growls at me and spits blood in my face from the cut he now has on his lip.

He glares at me and climbs up onto my chest to straddle me, holding my arms down with his knees as he continues to tie up my wrists to the headboard, making sure that he tightens the rope enough to irritate my skin and make it red. The pain isn't unbearable, but it is uncomfortable. If I move in the wrong way, it will give me rope burns.

He gets off my chest and starts stroking his long hard cock as he watches me try to get out of the ropes.

Laughing at my struggle, he says," You can't get out, Preciosa. The more you struggle, the more it will just hurt you."

I growl at him and snap my teeth at him. Sounding like a feral animal at this point.

Tony walks forward and gets up on the bed to straddle my waist. He flicks open his pocket knife and starts to spin it around in his hand, making a show of it before staring down at me with a sinister look in his eyes and a smile that cocks up just enough to make him look like the Joker from Batman. "Let's have a little fun, shall we, Preciosa?"

He slides the blade down my cheek, and I jerk away, causing the blade to nick my cheek in the process. A small trickle of blood starts to slide down my cheek to my neck as Tony continues to slide down, going between my breasts. He moves the blade to my right breast and circles the tip of the blade over my nipple; moving down, he cuts the lower part of my breast, and blood starts to slide down the side of my ribs.

"So pretty, bleeding for me like a good girl." He is trying to sound sexy, but it only makes me feel nauseous.

"I'm not your fucking good girl." I spit out. Hoping that the actual spit would hit him in the face. I start to pull against the rope, hoping it will loosen just enough for me to free one hand.

"Yes, you are, Preciosa. The more you struggle, the more you hurt yourself, and the more hurt you are, the more I get turned on."

He moves the blade to my left breast and cuts me again, this time a little longer and deeper than the other one. Blood pours out of the cut and down onto the bed.

"I'm going to play with you with my knife while I fuck that tight little cunt of yours and fill you up with my cum." He then bends down towards my ear and whispers, "So when the boss has his way with you, he can feel me in you." His face widens into another disturbing Joker grin.

I can feel the vomit rising to the surface of my throat just from his words. I try to swallow it down because I refuse to show weakness to this dumbass.

He starts to stroke his cock as he moves his ass up my body until he is leaning over my face. He grabs my cheeks to make me open my mouth and shoves his cock in, groaning in pleasure. I start to bite down on his dick, and he forcefully shoves his cock into the back of my mouth, causing me to gag. When my teeth aren't on him anymore, he pulls out.

He shakes his head at me as if I were a disobedient puppy. "Oh, no, no, no. We don't bite around here."

"Fuck you!" I yell at him as I keep trying to get free. I can feel my wrists burning as the rope digs into my skin. I know without even looking that I am going to have ugly bruises on my wrists from it.

"Oh, I plan to fuck you, Preciosa, now be a good girl and take this dick!" He groans the last bit out as he forcefully enters me. I am as dry as the Sahara desert, causing it to burn the whole time he enters me. I scream out, choking in pain.

"Scream for me, baby! It's music to my ears." Pulling almost all the way out of me and slamming in again. Tears are running down my face now, and I can't stop them even if I try.

Tony continued to thrust in and out of me while rubbing his knife over my body. He cuts me several more times on my stomach, thighs, arms, and the last one on my neck. If he had pushed a little bit harder, he would have hit my Carotid Artery straight on and killed me. Wouldn't that have been a treat? Because, at this point, I would rather be dead.

He lays down the knife on the bedside table, grabs my throat, and starts to cut off my air. With one last final thrust, he grunts, and I can feel the warmth of him coating my insides. The vomit that I have been holding in comes out, and it covers Tony. He laughs diabolically as if my vomiting turns him on even more. He starts to squeeze my throat harder. I now have no air at all and started to see stars in my vision.

I swear, when I get the chance, I am going to kill this fucker for what...

My final thought cut off before the oxygen loss caused me to pass out.

Chapter Thirty-Five

Alex

I go to my office to turn on the transmitter so no one can hear my call, and then I click on my grandfather's name on my phone.

"Lopez García," he answers on the second ring.

"Please tell me what I am hearing isn't true." I plead with him, hoping that Oliver and his dad are wrong, that my grandfather wouldn't be so cruel as to take the woman I am with for some twisted game.

"It all depends on what you are hearing; many people talk."

"Do you have a girl held hostage right now?" I am trying to sound as stern as possible, while also not giving away that Olivia is my weakness.

"Mi Nieto, I sell women. Of course, I have girls held hostage. I'm unsure of the exact number right now, but I can get Tony to give me the number and get back to you with it," he says nonchalantly as if he is having a normal conversation with someone on the street.

"No, you have one of the girls I have been dating. I want her back! Now! She is mine." I yell at him.

"Mi Nieto, you know I can't just get rid of my product. You have never shown concern for the family business or who is involved. Why now? Do you want to join and be part of the business? I can make you my right hand." He sounds fucking excited right now.

"First off, No. I do not want to be a part of this ghastly trade you deal in. I don't think it's right that you sell humans like cattle. Second, I don't believe you are selling Olivia. I believe you are holding her against her will because of her father." I am trying to keep my temper in check, but this man. Family or not. He is ready to get shot. I'm done playing these games with him. I want my girl back, and I want her back now.

"Ahhh." He says. "Olivia, that beautiful red-headed cop? Yes, she is here with me. You have such a feisty one there. But to clarify what you just said. yes, I will be selling her, just as I would any other woman I have. But I think I might play with this one a little bit first."

Did he just fucking say what I think he said? I am seeing red! He has my girl! He is talking about taking advantage of her and is acting like this is no big deal!

"I want her back! Now!" I yell into the phone.

"Mi Nieto, you need to stop yelling. I will not get rid of her until the auction is over. I am sorry to disappoint you. She is important to me and my business. So sorry. " Before I can reply, he hangs up.

I screamed and threw my phone against the wall. How could he fucking do that? How does he even sleep at night? I reach up and grab the roots of my hair and pull as hard as I can, trying to get any other pain to take over the pain in my heart. My breathing is ragged, and the tears start to fall. I stand up and punch the wall to get some of these emotions out so I can try to fucking think. The punch breaks the wall, causing the drywall to flow further from the fist-sized hole. How have I failed Olivia so badly? I need to find her. I need to think about where my grandfather would keep her so that I can get her back.

My spiraling is interrupted when I hear a knock on my door. I turn towards it, and Rachel's head pops in. Her hair is wet, and she is wearing one of my shirts that hangs down to her mid-thigh.

"I'm sorry to interrupt. I heard a scream and banging. I wanted to make sure you were okay." She smiles shyly.

I hold my arms out to her, and she walks into them without asking questions. I nuzzle my nose into her hair, inhale her scent, and try to relax a bit. This plan, Oliver and I have better fucking work. If not, I will lose Olivia, and I'm not sure I could handle that. I reach up and rub Rachel's hair, trying to soothe the rage simmering in my bones.

This is the calm before the storm that is about to wreak havoc on all of San Diego. I am that storm and will burn this whole planet to the ground for these women.

Chapter Thirty-Six

Rachel

I was getting out of the shower when I heard Alex yelling down the hall. I dried off my body as fast as possible and put on one of Alex's white shirts, which I had stolen from his dresser.

I tiptoed down the hall so no one would know I was walking to the office. I put my ear up to the door and listened for a minute.

"I want her back! NOW!" I hear Alex yell into the phone.

There is silence, then a scream, and something hitting the wall.

I know I shouldn't interrupt whatever is happening, but Alex helped me this morning with my nightmare, and I feel like I owe it to him to make sure he is okay.

I knock on the door and quietly open it. When I peek my head in, Alex pulls at his hair, looking completely defeated.

When he opened his arms to me, I knew all I could do was hug him and be there. Nothing I said or did would help him at that moment.

"Can I help in any way?" I say, looking up at him with soft eyes.

"No Muñeca. It's ok. I have to figure this out, and you have enough on your plate after everything that happened with Andrew's death..." He stops mid-sentence.

I looked up at him, shocked. "What do you mean after everything that happened with Andrew's death? What do you know?"

"Umm." That is all that comes out while avoiding eye contact.

I grab his face with my hands to make him look at me. "What do you know, Alex?"

A single tear falls down his cheek, and he looks at me. I wipe it away with my thumb, and he finally starts to speak. "I know that Andrew is dead. I'm not positive, but when I looked into it, no one came in or out of the house besides you and him. Which leads me to believe you could have possibly killed him."

My heart stops, and I start to breathe heavily. I can't even get words out right now.

"Hey, Rachel. Look at me, baby. It's ok. I'm not mad. I'm not scared. I am so proud of you. If you did kill him, I am so proud of you for finally standing up to him." He kisses my forehead.

Tears are streaming down my face now. He holds my face in his hands, wiping my tears with his thumbs.

"I don't understand how you don't care. I'm a monster. I killed a man. I stabbed him! How can you even look at me right now?" I put my hands on my face so he couldn't see me, as if it would hide what I had done.

Pulling my hands from my face, he grabbed his office chair, sat down on it, and pulled me onto his lap.

"Shhh. Shhhh. Baby, it's ok. You don't have to worry. I am not disgusted, mad, or embarrassed by you. The things I have seen in my life are worse than this. What you did is minor in comparison. I know it doesn't seem minor, but you did what you had to do. It was self-defense. You are a survivor." He is rubbing my head and soothing me.

I look up at him with tear-stained cheeks and red eyes. "Can I tell you something? It's not normal, but I need to say it, and you are the only person I trust right now."

He still has me in his grasp. "Anything Muñeca. You can always tell me anything."

"I would do it again." It comes out in a whisper. I am not sure he even heard what I said.

Grabbing my face, he makes me look at him, "Of course you would. You were defending yourself. That takes so much strength. I am in awe of you, Rachel. You are so fucking strong, baby. "

I look up at him and grab his face with my hands. We stare into each other's eyes while holding the other's face for a long minute. The stubble on his face feels scratchy on my hands in the best ways; his eyes are devouring me, and I never want to escape.

"No, Alex, you don't understand. I liked it. I liked the sound of the blade cutting his skin. I loved hearing the gurgling sound as he was trying to get air. And the metallic smell of the blood in the air turned me on." I let go of his face and buried my face in my hands. I am completely ashamed of what I am saying. I mean, for fuck sake, I am in school to be a Lawyer, and I am telling my boyfriend that I enjoyed murdering my ex.

Wait a minute. Boyfriend? Where did that come from?

I push the thought away for another time.

"Alex. I am just letting all my truths come out right now. I would do it again. I would kill for you. I would kill for Olivia. I would kill for everyone I care about. And worst of all, I would still sleep fine at night. I don't have nightmares about killing Andrew; I have nightmares about being raped by him."

Alex lets go of me and starts to laugh—not just any laugh, a full-belly laugh. He is bent over, trying to catch his breath from laughing so hard.

I cross my arms and stare at him. I don't know what he thinks is funny about what I just admitted.

After five minutes of tears running down Alex's face, he finally stopped laughing.

"Phew," he says, wiping his eyes. "That was great."

I raise my eyebrow at him. "Want to explain what was so funny?"

"You." That was all he could say before he started to laugh again.

"What exactly about what I said is oh so funny, Alex?" Now I am irritated, and all my attitude is coming out of my mouth.

He wipes the tears out of his eyes from laughing so hard again and grabs my hands.

"Baby, it's funny because I could tell you didn't feel bad when I picked you up at the park. I didn't know you killed Andrew then, but as soon as I put the two together, I could tell by the way you were acting that the actual killing didn't bother you at all." My eyes go big, and my jaw drops. That is not what I expected to come out of his mouth.

"Okay, now that everything about me is out of the way. Want to tell me who you were screaming at and who you want back?" I cross my arms and pop my hip out to the side.

"So..." He trails off like he doesn't want to say anything. I stand there patiently waiting for him to spit it out.

"So Olivia has been taken." I try to keep my face neutral, but I feel my heart sink into my stomach.

"Taken?" I feel the rage starting to bubble. I don't know who thinks they can take my girl, but they have another thing coming for them.

My Girl? Another thing to add to the list to figure out later. When did I get so attached to Alex and Olivia?

"First. Who took her? Second. Where did they take her?" I start to pace the room, hoping it will help calm me down.

Alex grabs my arms to get me to stop pacing and look at him.

"This won't be easy to hear, and it's a long story. I don't know where Olivia is. But I know my grandfather has her."

Chapter Thirty-Seven

Olivia

I woke up in a clean bed. I am untied and alone. I feel around since my head is pounding, and opening my eyes seems impossible. There is no vomit, no cum, no blood... But there are rose petals? They feel like rose petals. I sit up with a fuzzy brain again and try to look around. I am wearing a pair of grey sweatpants and a white shirt. Both are so big that I am swimming in them. Tony must have drugged me after his fun last night.

It takes a minute for my eyes to adjust. When everything finally clears up, I see a vase with at least a dozen red roses on the nightstand to my left. Scattered all over the bed and floor are red rose petals. Is this Tony? Why would he have his way with me last night to try to romance me today? Nothing is adding up.

I get out of bed and notice that I am not chained to anything. I can thank the Lord for that. I walk to the door and try to open it, but as I suspected, it is locked from the outside. I need time to think of a plan, and I do my best planning in the shower.

The water is extremely hot, which I like, and there is even a little bench for me to sit on. I let the water flow down my body, trying to wash away what happened with Tony and the nasty feeling I have from being in this place.

I hear the door open with a loud bang.

"Preciosa! Where are you? The boss wants to see you right now!" I hear Tony yelling, most likely still standing in the doorway. Groaning loudly, I turn off the water and grab my towel off the hook.

"I'll be out in a second. I am getting dressed," I yell back at him. You can hear heavy footsteps running, and the bathroom door slams open, shaking the walls. Tony looks me up and down with heat in his eyes, and my stomach turns. This man staring at me is the absolute most disgusting human being ever. His greasy, slicked-back black hair and his yellow-tinted teeth. He has a scar running down his left cheek. The only thing he has going for him is his muscles. The man is ripped. But that doesn't fix the other problems there.

"Don't mind me, Preciosa; I will just sit here and watch." I roll my eyes and go back to the room to dry off. I get back into the sweats and T-shirt I woke up in since Tony sliced through my other clothes. I can feel Tony's eyes on me the whole time, never leaving my tits or ass. Once I am dressed, I turn to Tony and stare at him. "Are we going or what?"

Tony stands quickly, opens the door, and walks me down a long, bright hallway. At least they don't have me in the dungeon anymore. Once we reach the end of the hall, I am face to face with two massive, dark-colored oak doors. Tony knocks on the door and then pokes his head in slightly. He says something in Spanish that I didn't catch, opens the door wider and then ushers his hand for me to enter. Walking in, I take in the room. The walls are grey, and there are paintings on the wall; some are landscapes, and others are naked women—a red velvet couch to the right side of a giant oak desk. Lopez García sits in a large black leather chair behind the desk, smoking a cigar, the smell of it floating through the room.

Lopez García looks up from what looks like a folder on his desk and smiles at me. "Come in, Olivia. We have much to talk about. My grandson gives his regards." He motions to the red velvet couch. I sit on the couch and get comfy, crossing my arms around my chest. If I am going to have a shit time here and most likely die, I might as well make myself comfy and give attitude until the bitter end.

"And who would your grandson be?"

I look at him with hatred as he laughs at me. His laugh was deep and loud, echoing off the walls.

"Alejandro Lopez García. But you may know him as Alex García."

I try to keep my emotions neutral, but fail completely when my heart sinks into my stomach. Alex is his grandson? Does Alex know I'm here? Was he involved in this? This had to be a setup.

My head is swimming with questions.

"He called me this morning, demanding I let you go, that you are his." He says matter-of-factly.

"So, why am I still here? Why didn't you release me into his custody?" I say, undoing my arms from my chest and trying to make myself look as relaxed as possible. He doesn't need to know my thoughts.

"Well, you see, sweet Olivia, I don't answer to my grandson. I also don't answer to your dad or brother, either. I have you here with me because you are an asset in helping me achieve what I want. And sweet girl, I always get what I want." He smiles at me as he finishes his sentence.

"Ok, cool. So you don't answer to anyone. Awesome. But what does my dad and brother have to do with the cartel? What do you want from them? From our phone call, you mentioned that my dad didn't agree to a deal. What deal?"

"I wanted to get my trade business going in New York. I know your family does business in New York, and your dad refused to work with me to grant access to the ports. They are under the Irish, and I am not trying to start a whole war."

My head is swimming. I don't understand. Under the Irish? What does that even mean? My confusion must have been written all over my face because another chuckle comes from Lopez GarcÍa, and I can also hear Tony chuckling behind me.

"Sweet girl. You didn't know your dad was in charge of the Irish mafia in New York?"

What on earth is this man talking about?

His laugh booms. "My sweet girl apparently doesn't know what daddy and brother are doing behind her back." He walks towards me, runs his knuckles down my face, and grabs my jaw hard to make me look up at him. I try to jerk out of his grip and push him away.

"Oh, come on, dear. You think I would leave you untied if I didn't feel confident handling you?" He grabbed my chin again, but it was harder, turning my head from side to side as if he were examining his product.

A soft hmmm comes from his voice, and then he grabs the collar of my shirt and rips it apart. My jaw dropped, and my face reddened because he made that look easy, and now I am completely exposed again.

He bends down and kisses my neck.

"STOP!" I yell and push him again.

"No." He says back to me. I try to fight him off, and he snaps his fingers and steps back from me. Then, I am being lifted to stand in front of Tony, who spins me around and cuffs my wrists behind me.

Fucking great.

"Now, sweet girl, are you going to behave for me?" He says sweetly to me while tracing his fingers down my arm.

"Fuck you!" I spit at him.

Tony and Lopez García laugh when he grabs me by my arm and shoves me onto his desk.

"No, sweet Olivia. You see, I will be the one fucking you." Lopez García whispers in my ear, then licks up my neck.

"Mmmm. Tony was right; you do taste good. Let's see if you feel as good as he says you do, also." He brings his hands to my front, one hand grabbing my breast and the other holding my pussy through my clothes. I wrapped my leg around him to get his knee to buckle and allow me to get the upper advantage, but when his knee buckled, he fell on top of me, crushing me into the desk more.

"Impatient, are we?" He growls in my ear. "Don't worry, sweet girl. I got you. I will take care of all of your needs."

He starts sliding his hand up my back and wraps his hand around the back of my neck, pushing my head into the desk so I stay in place as he undoes his belt. He rips it through the loops with a whoosh and then places it down on the desk next to my head. He undoes the button and zipper on his pants, lowering them down. Then, reaching for my hips with his free hand, he pulls down my sweatpants.

"Your ass is absolutely stunning." He smacks my ass and sends a sting running up my spine, causing me to grunt in response.

"Oh, did you like that, sweet girl?" He asks while he rubs the red mark that I know is forming on my ass.

"No. I fucking didn't. Let me go, you disgusting pervert!" I try to kick back but end up just kicking the air. I get another smack to the ass in the same spot as last time, so the sting is even worse. I can't help the hiss in response. Before there is any time to think, he shoves into me.

"FUCK!" I scream. The pain erupts everywhere. I am not wet; there is no lube, and it feels like sandpaper scraping the inside of me. He keeps thrusting in and out of me, causing the dry friction to rub more. I think I am getting the equivalent of a rug burn in my pussy!

Chapter Thirty-Eight

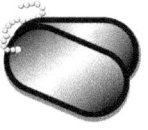

Alex

"Hey, Rach, I have got to go to the airport," I yelled down the hall at her. She was getting dressed in real clothes instead of pajamas, so we could come up with a plan to get Olivia back.

Rachel comes out of the bedroom, wearing black leather pants, a white shirt, a leather jacket, and bright red stiletto heels. Her makeup is done, including lipstick that matches her heels, and her blonde hair is pulled up into a high ponytail.

Instantly my cock starts to get hard, having a mind of its own. I would take her back to my room if the situation weren't so serious and time-sensitive. We had to leave now, but damn, she looks sexy as hell.

"Ready to go, handsome?" she says, walking past me. She pats my chest lightly as she passes me and goes down the stairs. I turn and follow, grabbing the keys as we head to the garage and get into the black lifted Toyota 4Runner I purchased after deployment.

When I get into the driver's seat, I look over at Rachel, and she is pulling a knife out of her bra and starts to flip it in her hand.

"Where the fuck did that come from?" I ask her in shock. She just pulled out a fucking knife like it's no big deal.

"My bra." She replied nonchalantly with a shrug, like it was completely normal.

"How many knives do you have on you right now?" I ask. I am honestly scared to know the answer, but I need to know how armed she is.

"I only have five on me. Why?" She raises an eyebrow at me as if questioning my question.

"Good lord, woman! Are you trying to kill me? Why didn't you tell me you were armed? Why are you armed?" I start firing off questions at her. She grabs the knife and licks the blade, looking sexy as hell and psycho all at once.

"No, I am not trying to kill you, Alex. If I were, you would already be dead. And I love you too much for that. Also, I am armed because we don't know what we're getting into. We don't know who Oliver is; if I am not mistaken, you remember my past just as well as I do. I also don't plan on getting captured, either. I do plan on killing whoever decided it was a great idea to take my girl, and now that you know that I don't feel bad for killing people, I decided that I don't have to hide that side of me anymore." She continues to mess with her blades like it's completely normal.

"Wait a minute. First... Did you say you loved me?"

She facepalms her forehead and sighs. "Yes, Alex. Now, let's get to the real situation at hand. Get Oliver so that we can rescue Olivia?" My face flushes with her admission, and my heart squeezes. She said she loved me. I wasn't expecting that, especially with everything that has been going on. I know that if I had to label my feelings, they would be the closest thing to love I have ever had.

Ten minutes later, we pulled into the airport, and Oliver was standing next to his jet with his duffle bag slung over his shoulders. He looked exactly like a male version of Olivia. It was honestly kind of creepy. If I were gay, I would absolutely go for him. But I am straighter than straight. So it's good that there is a female version of him. That is all mine—well, not exactly all mine—but mine and Rachel's.

I get out of my car and walk up to Oliver. I'm sticking my hand out for a handshake. "Hey man, I am Alex."

"Oliver." He returns the handshake but gives me a questioning look.

Alrighty then.... I guess we are on questionable terms. What the fuck did I do to this fucker?

"Do you know where my sister is?" he asks, scouting the area for anything that could potentially go wrong. I know that look because I do it, too.

"I have ideas, but nothing is coming back solid." My guys have been searching, but I have all of my grandfather's guys against me.

When we get to the car, Rachel moves to the backseat, holding the tip of her knife on her finger and twisting it in circles. It is not hard enough to break the skin, but it makes Oliver look at me and lift an eyebrow, questioning my sanity. I want to tell him he has no idea what he just walked into, but I keep my mouth shut.

"Hey, Rach. This is Oliver. Olivia's twin brother." I introduce them.

Rachel looks up from the blade and gets an ear-to-ear smile. "Hey! I am Rachel! I'm Olivia's girl." She said, bouncing in her seat to move forward so she could reach Oliver and wrap him in a hug. This time, a confused look crossed Oliver's face; all I could do was smile and shrug.

"Well, aren't you the cutest little psycho I have ever met?" He replies with a slight chuckle.

Rachel shrugs as if it's no big deal. "Some call me psycho; I call it being protective. So basically the same thing." She hops back to her seat and starts to play with her knife again. "So, who are we killing for taking my girl?" She says without looking up from her knife.

Oliver looks over at me and raises an eyebrow again. This dude has no idea who his sister has in her corner.

"So tell me what you know," I demand from Oliver, ignoring Rachel's question because mine will answer hers.

Oliver tells me about his family being the Irish mafia and how my grandfather wanted shipments to come into New York. So, he was trying to create a plan with Olivia's dad, but the O'Connors didn't want to make a deal in the skin trade. He then goes on to tell me about the phone call my grandfather had with his dad. Olivia's voice was shaky, but she seemed to be well from what they could hear, and he had been looking for anything on Olivia's whereabouts since that call.

We pull up to the house, and as soon as I park the car, Rachel runs out and up the stairs. When she comes back down, she is changed into a pencil skirt, a flowing white button-up blouse, and her signature red heels. Her hair is pulled back in a twisty bun thing. "Where are you going?"

"I have to go to the office. I got a text from Katie saying someone was at the office for me," she says. Damn, the girl can kill someone without blinking an eye, then turn around and fight for justice in the courtroom. It's like a switch she can turn on or off. I am grateful we have her on our side in this war that is about to happen. I don't want to be on the receiving end of her knives.

I lean in and kiss her. "Let me know when you make it to the office, and let me know if you need my help with anything," I say, pressing another kiss on her head.

"I'm a big girl, Alex; I can handle myself. Also! One of your girls is a hotshot Lawyer, remember?" She pats my cheek, winks at me, and walks to the garage.

Oliver looks at me with another questioning look. "I am guessing there is more that I need to learn."

I pour two glasses of whiskey from the wet bar in my office and hand him one. I swallow a healthy drink and say, "More than you think."

I gestured for him to sit down so we could come up with a plan. We can pass the information on to Rachel when she gets home.

"Alright Lopez García." Alex looks up from his whiskey.

"I'm gonna stop you right there! Don't call me that! EVER! It's either Alex or García." I say sternly with a no-bullshit look on my face. I fucking hate being called by my grandfather's name.

"Got it. My bad, dude." Oliver holds his hands up in surrender.

"No problem. I am just not very fond of my grandfather, and that's his name, not mine." I take a healthy drink of my whiskey.

Oliver clapped his hands together and leaned his elbows onto his legs. "Alright, Alex. Let's save my sister."

Chapter Thirty-Nine

Rachel

I park the 4Runner in my office spot. It's Friday, and I usually have Fridays off, but my assistant called to tell me that a guy in the office was looking for me and wouldn't leave without speaking to me. So, of course, I put on my most professional business outfit, but I decided against wearing a suit jacket. This blouse looks good enough without it.

I get in the elevator, press the 40 button, and head up to the office. I felt around my body to count each knife I had on my person. I only bought three because the pencil skirt is too tight to conceal more, but I don't go anywhere without my knives. I learned the hard way with Andrew that people are shitty, I refuse to be a victim again.

The ding of the elevator brings my attention back to the office. I enter with the click of my heels on the pristine floor, walking up to the front desk and saying hello to Cheryl as I make my way towards my office. I can see Katie sitting at her desk outside my office with a fake smile. Something feels off, and her facial expression tells me all I need to know. That's when I saw it. Andrew's oldest brother, Tyler, is here. He sits at about 6'7"; he has the same bright red hair as Andrew. Unlike Andrew, though, he was fit; his biceps were as big as my head. Well fuck. Here is my past catching up to me.

I walk up to my office. "Tyler," I say in my most unenthused voice. "Rachel! I have been waiting for you, " he says in his deep, gravelly voice.

"So I have been told. Please come in and have a seat," I say as I walk in and motion to the chair in front of my desk. He sits in the chair and looks at me, concerned. Well, that's unexpected.

"What can I help you with, Tyler?" I ask, looking him up and down. It has always amazed me how Andrew was hit with the ugly stick compared to his brothers. Andrew is also the youngest of five brothers, so maybe his mom ran out of good-looking genes when she got to him.

"I am going to be blunt with you, Rachel. I haven't heard from or seen Andrew in almost a month. The last time I heard from him, he said he was in trouble and needed money. Unfortunately, as much as I love my brother, I refuse to condone his bad habits, and he needs to pay off his debts on his own. I am tired of being the punching bag for his mistakes."

"I completely agree with you. He was in a mess that he wouldn't tell me about. The last time I saw him, he told me we had to leave. He wouldn't tell me where we were going or why. I refused to go with him, and he got mad. I left and called my friend to come pick me up because Andrew was starting to get physical with me. I haven't seen him since." The partial lie slid right out of my mouth with ease. I wasn't completely lying, though, so that's probably why it seemed so easy. Tyler looks at me with pity, and my stomach drops. I fucking hate pity.

"I am so sorry he got physical with you, Rachel; you didn't deserve that. I wish I could have stopped him." I scoff at him.

"I know I didn't deserve it, but it also wasn't your responsibility to deal with him. But, if I am being frank, you don't even know half of what I went through, Tyler. Andrew killed our baby! When I told him I was pregnant. He kicked me into a brick building. He would beat me until I lost consciousness! He blamed me for everything that went wrong with him, no matter what it was. Even when he had people coming at him for money, he was mad at me for it. Like I was the one who was involved with the people, or I sent them to come after him. I didn't deserve any of it and am just starting to realize that. He deserved whatever fate he got! Someone he owed probably got to him and killed him for his debt, or had him strung up in a basement. Truthfully, I don't even care, he was in a bunch of sketchy shit. I mean, for fuck sake, he tried to sell me to pay off his debt at one point. Like I was disposable." I am screaming at this point. I don't even care. The whole office could be standing at my door, and I would give no fucks.

Tyler's face turns ghostly white as he takes in the words coming out of my mouth. "You were pregnant?"

He asked. Out of everything I just told him, the only thing he cares about is me being pregnant. I am the one who lost the baby. I am the one who still has nightmares about it all. The baby at least passed, not having to deal with an abusive dad. The baby passed, knowing its mom loved it more than anything else in this world.

"Seriously?" I pinch the bridge of my nose, and I sigh at him. "Out of everything I just said to you, all you recall is that I was pregnant?" As soon as the question leaves my mouth, you can see the fact that he realized he fucked up.

"No, no, no, not at all, Rachel. I was shocked to find out that I was going to be an uncle. I didn't know." He stutters over his words, trying to backpedal his mistake.

"Yes, an uncle. To a dead baby because your brother kicked me into a wall of a building! And no, you didn't know because the baby died before I had the chance to announce it because the father got pissed." This catches his attention. ▨

"I'm sorry that happened to you, Rachel. I know Andrew was raised better than that. I personally made sure to teach him not to disrespect women. I don't know what happened. He was a good kid. I guess the thirteen-year age difference doesn't help because I was out of the house when he was growing up." He looks sincere, but I know how his brother is a piece of shit. I don't know him or the other three brothers well enough to judge them, but I do know Andrew. I know Andrew like the back of my hand. He made sure I knew every little detail he liked.

"Alright, now that you know what happened between Andrew and me," I say through ragged breaths, still trying to lower my heart rate and rage, trying to keep the tears and grief at bay as the emotions flood through me. They are becoming unbearable; I need to hurry up this meeting.

"What else can I help you with, Tyler?" I say through a slight sob that I am hoping he doesn't catch on to it.

I'm ready to get back home and figure out the plan the guys made. I need to get my mind off my baby and back on getting Olivia back so I can feel complete again. Who would have known that she would have started to mean so much to me in such a short amount of time? At least I have my new little family to hold me together when I fall apart because, after this conversation with Tyler, I am going to need to cry or stab someone.

"Um, yeah. I will need a lawyer for some... um.. business that I am... um... attending to." This doesn't sound suspicious at all... I roll my eyes at him.

"Okay, I need to know what kind of business this is and what you need my assistance with, but I am going to suggest that we conduct these meetings outside of my office in the future." I don't mind helping Tyler, but I will not go down for this family again. His chances are limited, but he gets a chance because he has never wronged me. But that doesn't mean that I don't have my eyes on the brothers. One wrong move, and I will wipe out the entire Starr brothers' generation.

Chapter Forty

Olivia

Tony carries me to my room after the "meeting" with Lopez García. If you could even call it a meeting. I got told that the guy I had been seeing knew I was here, captured by his grandfather, then got raped.

Alex knew I was investigating the Cartel. He didn't seem to be trying to stop me, but he wasn't trying to help me either. I don't know what to think about Alex, but that is a problem for another time. Right now, I need to focus on getting myself and the other victims out of here.

While here, I will try to help as many victims as possible. I can also find out where they are and who is actually holding them hostage. I assume they are at some sort of warehouse, but there is no telling. What I do know is that I refuse to let those victims have the same things that are happening to me happen to them.

Tony jerks me around as we round the corner of the hallway leading to my room. When we walk in, a box with a note on top is on my bed. Great, that's just what I need. More surprises. "Tony, what the hell is on my bed?" I asked him with no emotion in my voice at all.

"It's a gift from the boss. He told me to make sure that you get dressed and come down to the banquet hall by 7."

I looked at the clock and saw that it was already 6:15 p.m. "What am I getting ready for?" I looked up at him, hoping to understand what was happening.

"Boss is having a party tonight and wants to show you off. So get dressed so we can head down and enjoy the night."

A party? This mother fucker captured me, raped me, and now expects me to entertain at a party? I don't even have enough energy to get out of bed half the time.

Tony sets me down, and I walk to my bed and pick up the note.

PUT THIS ON, AND DO YOUR HAIR AND MAKE-UP. NO PANTIES OR BRA

That's it? Nothing else on the note? I stare at the card for a while longer, as if something on it is going to change. I noticed the similarity in the handwriting compared to the note Alex left me. The thought alone makes me crumple up the note and throw it across the room with a scream. I can't believe Alex is behind all of this.

Fuck this
Fuck him
Fuck my feelings I still have for him.
Fuck it all

I open the box and see a strapless, sparkling emer-ald-green dress. It is beautiful. I pick it up and hold it up to myself. Green is the perfect color for my pale skin and red hair. I look in the box and find a pair of black heels at the bottom, along with a velvet box next to it. My breath hitches at the anticipation and irritation of what is in that velvet box.

I lay the dress on my bed, pull the shoes out, and set them next to it. Finally, I get the nerve to pick up the velvet box and open it. Inside are a diamond ten-nis bracelet and a matching necklace. This bracelet has more diamonds than I have ever seen in one place other than a jewelry store.

Regardless of my family apparently being the Irish mafia, we lived a very modest lifestyle. I am assuming that was part of the act to keep me oblivious to what was happening right under my nose. I was raised to be humble and to appreciate what I had. I have never held something so expensive before, and honestly, I am scared to even wear it. What if it falls off, and I lose it? That would be my luck. I want to throw the bracelet across the room and break it. But I can't bring myself to do that. The jewelry is not the reason I have blood running down my legs.

My soul is in pieces; my world is shattering around me.

I grab my chest, my heart physically aching from the betrayal.

Forty-five minutes later, I am in the emerald dress that hugs every one of my curves just right. My red hair cascades in ringlets down my back, and my makeup is just right. The diamond necklace hangs from my neck, and these black heels are already killing my feet. Not a teardrop or blood in sight.

I walk up to Tony, sitting in the chair beside my door, playing a game on his phone. He is completely oblivious to anything around him, including me standing right in front of him.

"Tony. Are you ready?" I ask. He damn near jumps out of his skin, and I can't help but laugh so hard I am bent over, grabbing my stomach.

"You know, for such a big guy, you scare easily. How does that work with you working for the Cartel?" Tony's eyes are daggers. If looks could kill, I would be dead on the spot.

"Got it, big guy. No more jokes." I say to him as I pat his chest and walk past him. Mumbling under my breath, "Fucking *pussy*," as I walk away, my heels clicking on the ground the whole way.

A whole party is in full swing downstairs when we finally get to the banquet hall. There have to be over two hundred people here, and they all look to be upper-class with their fancy dresses and perfectly tailored suits.

What is the occasion? Mentally, I smack myself in the forehead. Why do I even care? I am being held captive here; hundreds, if not thousands, of men, women, and children need my help, and I am worried about what occasion it is to have a party. What in the actual fuck is wrong with me?

Tony walks me up to Lopez García, "sweet girl. I am so glad you could join us tonight." He says as he walks up next to me, leaning to kiss my cheek. I flinch in reaction, and he puts his hand on the small of my back. I want to break his hand for touching me, but I can't afford to make a scene here, so I just keep my mouth shut.

"Let me introduce you to everyone, dear. They have been impatiently waiting for your arrival so they could meet you." I rolled my eyes before he could see. This guy is so full of shit, but once again, I keep my mouth shut for the sake of my life. After a trip around the banquet hall, I met more people than not, and I hoped there would be no quiz after this because I didn't think I could remember one name. We finally end up at a table in the front of the room next to the stage.

I am gestured to sit down as Lopez García walks towards a stage. A man in a waiter's suit comes up and pours me a glass of water, and I take a sip, wishing it were something with more alcohol content in it, but I guess it's for the best of me to stay clear-headed during this whole thing. I have no idea what to expect at this party and need a level head to handle any possibility that may be thrown my way.

"Good evening, everyone." Lopez García's voice booms through the speaker. "Tonight is a very special night, and I have a surprise for you." You can hear the whisper of wonder throughout the crowd. I try to sit here, as if I am paying complete attention to Lopez García, and not memorize every square inch of this house to find the easiest exit.

"Usually, my annual auctions are a little more of the mixed variety, if you know what I mean." The crowd gives a soft chuckle. Am I the only one who finds that comment disgusting? But I assume you can't be friends with Lopez García and not like holding people against their will to do your bidding.

"But this year, not only will I have the usual product up for auction, but I will also have a beautiful woman who is quite unique up for auction tonight as well." The crowd starts to murmur again and looks around to find the woman that Lopez García is talking about. I am also guilty of looking around for this woman. If I have a chance, I might see if there is a way to get her out of here safely before they try to get her up on stage.

When I see the shuffle of black suits behind me, the hairs on the back of my neck stand up. And that's when it hits me.

I AM THE WOMAN.

I am the surprise that will be put up on that stage.

I get up as fast as the stupid-ass heels will let me and turn to try to run out of the room before I can get brought up to the stage, but at that exact moment, Tony wraps his arms around me.

I started punching Tony in any spot I could reach. I hear some grunts, but he doesn't loosen his grip.

"Tony, Stop! Get your hands off of me!" I screamed at him. Everyone in the banquet hall has turned to face us.

"Don't worry, Preciosa, we can still play after you are sold." He says in my ear with a growl. I fling my head back and get a satisfied crunch of his nose. "Fuck! You broke my nose bitch!" He yells at me. You can hear all the comments coming from the crowd.

"She is a feisty one."

"I wouldn't mind a piece of that."

"I wish Lopez always brought these types of women instead of the ugly ones and kids; I would buy more often."

Tony finally gets me up on the stage, and there is an evil grin on Lopez García's face. "Don't worry, sweetheart, you will make someone very happy, just like you did me." I shiver at the admission.

I look out into the crowd; honestly, every face I met earlier now looks different. Men are rubbing their hands together and licking their lips at me; women are looking at me like a piece of meat. It's as if they took off their 'normal' mask and became a predator. It makes my stomach get nauseous.

"Let's get this show on the road, shall we?" Lopez García says. I look at him like he has lost his damn mind. I am not a show. Fuck how can I get out of this? There has to be a way out of this building, even though

Lopez García and his goons are hovering. I'm wiggling a little to judge the grip Tony has on me. It's solid but not unbreakable.

So with that thought and courage from who knows where, I try to get out of Tony's grip. That is when he tightens his grip on me, and I feel the cold metal of handcuffs tightening on my wrist. Well, this just got a hell of a lot more complicated. I swing my head to the left, trying to make contact with someone, and all I see is another big bulky dude in a tux, like Tony, glaring at me as he tightens the cuffs one more notch, making it grip of the cuffs on my wrists uncomfortable, and if I move, my wrist, they will end up with marks.

"Don't you dare move! The marks on your wrists will make your new Master very upset." The other dude whispered into my ear. Tony shoves me to the middle of the stage and nods at Lopez García. Never letting go of my arms. Damn pussy has to put cuffs on me and still hold both of my arms in place. I rolled my eyes before anyone could see me.

"Well, Ladies and Gentlemen. That was a bit dramatic. I apologize for that. This here is Olivia. Not only can you tell that she is a fiery redhead, but she is also a dear Irish Mafia Princess. Her family is the O'Connor family in New York; they hold the biggest gun trading on the East Coast." He says it with such enthusiasm and charisma that I can see how this man persuades these people.

"She sits five feet five inches tall and is a solid one hundred and twenty pounds, not an ounce of fat on this woman, ladies and gentlemen. She works for the San Diego Police Department. So, as you can see, our little mafia princess is straddling both sides of the law. Imagine what else she could be straddling." He says with a chuckle, and the whole room chuckles and murmurs their agreement.

"Ok, now for the good parts." Lopez García says, grabbing my arm and spinning me around. As Tony loosened his grip so Lopez García could spin me, I tried to knee him in the balls and run, but this man, I swear, has balls of steel because he didn't even flinch when I made contact. He just tsked at me and grabbed my arms tighter.

Lopez García comes up behind me, grabs the bottom of my dress, and pulls it up. I spread my legs out so he couldn't move them any further. He bends toward my ear and whispers, "Don't worry, dear. There is a reason I chose this dress for you."

Tony grabs a knife from the sheath on his belt, puts the blade between my breasts, and cuts down the center of the dress. My cheeks flare red with anger as I try to grab the opening and forget my hands are cuffed behind my back. The sudden movement caused my wrists to split open. I feel the trickle of blood running down my hands and dripping off my fingers.

"No! Stop!" I yelled as I tried to move so he couldn't cut any more of my dress, which was stupid on my part because it caused his knife to shift and cut a line from my sternum down my stomach. The dark rage in Tony and Lopez García's faces intensifies, becoming terrifying.

"Look what you did, you fucking stupid girl!" Lopez García growls, then slaps me across the face. My head snaps to the side, and I feel the bruise forming on my cheek. The whole crowd gasps at the smack.

As soon as I catch my barring, I turn to Lopez García and spit the blood pooling in my mouth at his face. He gets a sinister grin on his face as he wipes off the blood and spit, then grabs the two halves of my dress and rips it the rest of the way down, throwing it to the side so I am now in nothing but my heels and jewelry.

"Alright, ladies and gentlemen, the last of the viewing before we start the bidding." Lopez García says, turning back towards the crowd.

Tony pushes my head down so I bend at the waist, and he kicks my legs to spread me open more. The crowd starts to comment on me. The worst part is that it is loud, and they talk as if I am not even here to hear them.

"Look at that pussy. It looks tight as fuck."

"She is a brat that I would like to get hold of."

"I wonder what all she has done with her tight ass."

I feel completely exposed and defeated. I don't even have the willpower or fight in me anymore. My breathing hitches, and a single tear falls down my face.

Tony lifts me back up and turns me around to show the crowd my tits and the front of my vagina, which has not been shaved since I went out with Alex.

"Oh, look at her pubs; they are as red as her hair. I can't wait to dive into that." A guy in the front says.

"She has some nice tits!" A girl comments.

"Can we start the bidding already?" I hear a male further back in the crowd.

"Alright, ladies and Gentlemen, we will start the bidding at thirty-five thousand dollars. Do I hear someone for thirty-five?" Lopez García says.

"Thirty-five," the guy in the front, who said he liked my pubes, says out, raising his little fan-looking thing with a number on it.

"Forty," I hear from a female.

"Fifty," I hear another female say.

The numbers keep going up. Eventually, we reach three hundred fifty thousand dollars. I don't know how a non-virgin would go for that much. But it seems like I am worth something around here. It's disgustingly flattering that someone would pay that much for me. Then again, these are the same people who also willingly buy children, so I really shouldn't be so shocked.

"One million dollars," I hear yelled from the back of the room. My jaw dropped. Who on earth just said that? It can't be real! There is no way that Lopez García will say no to that. At this point, I am as good as sold. I can't see who it is, but I can hear everyone in the crowd start to whisper to each other and talk about this guy who bid so much and the woman he is with.

"SOLD! For One Million Dollars to the gentlemen in the back!" Lopez García is basically salivating at the mouth when he is speaking. I glance at the crowd before being pulled backstage. I looked up and saw two figures walking towards the stage.

Alex and Rachel... My heart falls to my stomach. My heart flutters in excitement and aches from the betrayal. Rachel looks pissed and ready to kill everyone in sight, and Alex looks neutral like he doesn't have a care in the world. Fucking shocker; when he was behind all of this.

I hear the low rumble of Alex's voice over all the chaos.

"She comes with me!"

That's the end for now....

Want more of Olivia, Rachel, and Alex?

Find more in the next book of the Lovers in Crossfire series, *He is Ours*.

You can pre-order here

https://a.co/d/oofkSFO

Acknowledgements

To my wonderful husband, whose unwavering love has been my greatest strength. Your support has carried me through every challenge I have faced. Thank you for being my rock.

To my incredible children, biggest cheerleaders—your joy inspire me every day to keep moving forward.

To Kayla, Mel &Luci, Thank you for being the other part of my brain cell, keeping my ideas flowing when my brain said no and for not giving up on me when I wanted quit.

About the author

Rebekah Lynn is a Navy veteran, a devoted wife, and the mother of two spirited boys who keep life adventurous and full of laughter.

Nestled in the stunning Pacific Northwest, she finds joy in the great outdoors—whether it's hiking rugged trails, camping under the stars, or simply soaking in the beauty of nature with her family.

When she's not chasing boys or braving the elements, Rebekah carves out quiet moments for herself—often with a good book in hand and a heart full of stories waiting to be told. Her writing is infused with honesty, resilience, and a deep appreciation for life's everyday magic.

Rebekah Lynn's social media links!